To E.,

Enjoy the book. Hope to break you at the table. I only hope I'm half as talented at writing as you are with your music.

Don Darrin

Donald A. Dunn

The Enchanted Planet

Don Darrin

Bloomington, IN  Milton Keynes, UK

AuthorHouse™
1663 Liberty Drive, Suite 200
Bloomington, IN 47403
www.authorhouse.com
Phone: 1-800-839-8640

AuthorHouse™ UK Ltd.
500 Avebury Boulevard
Central Milton Keynes, MK9 2BE
www.authorhouse.co.uk
Phone: 08001974150

© 2006 Don Darrin. All rights reserved.

No part of this book may be reproduced, stored in a retrieval system, or transmitted by any means without the written permission of the author.

First published by AuthorHouse 9/13/2006

ISBN: 1-4259-4850-2 (sc)

Library of Congress Control Number: 2006906028

Printed in the United States of America
Bloomington, Indiana

This book is printed on acid-free paper.

This book is dedicated to my father,

Charles A. Darrin.

He is the inspiration for almost everything I do.
I miss him and wish we could have had
more time to spend together.

Contents

Chapter One: War Of The Worlds	1
Chapter Two: Recruiting	11
Chapter Three: Reunions	25
Chapter Four: Trip To The City	37
Chapter Five: Lift Off	51
Chapter Six: The Planet	59
Chapter Seven: Exploration	65
Chapter Eight: The Dambroo	81
Chapter Nine: Chores	89
Chapter Ten: Once Bitten	101
Chapter Eleven: The Pocala	117
Chapter Twelve: The Collector	143
Chapter Thirteen: The Journey North	159
Chapter Fourteen: Pondera Patoona	171
Chapter Fifteen: Gunallo	193
Chapter Sixteen: Relaxation	209
Chapter Seventeen: Shondo Waxanadu	221
Chapter Eighteen: Consequences	233
Chapter Nineteen: The Return Of Evil	245
Chapter Twenty: Return To Earth	257

Chapter One:
War Of The Worlds

1

As the long black limo rolled down the country road in central New York, there was a peaceful silence from the back seat. Sara sat there next to her father with a feeling of happiness. She glanced over at him sitting there in his dark suit. *'What a fine businessman,'* she thought. Her father owns a successful chain of car dealerships. He works all the time. He didn't work for the money; it was just in his nature. He certainly didn't need the money. He won the New York Lottery fifteen years ago. He invested a good portion of his 98 million dollars in stocks and made an even bigger fortune. A large sum of that went into a trust fund for Sara who would receive it when she turned 21. Last week on her 21st birthday, they went to the city together to have her funds transferred to her own account.

Sara was happy for her father. *'He will finally get the vacation he deserves,'* she thought as she looked over at him. He was going to fly to Africa. It was the break he needed from his work-filled life. Malcolm Smith was a worker. Sara on the other hand has never had to work. She has had everything handed to her.

Malcolm looked over at Sara with her fiery red hair and light complexion. "I'm going to miss you sweetheart," he said.

"I know dad."

"Are you sure you don't want to join me?" he asked her.

"I'm sure dad," she said. "I have to figure my life out. I'm twenty-one years old now and I've always needed you. This three weeks without you are exactly what I need."

"Maybe you're right honey," he said as he sighed.

2

The car slowed as it reached the entrance to the Allison Smith Memorial Airport. Malcolm had named it after his wife, who died of cancer when Sara was eight.

"Where is George?" Sara asked.

"He should already be here. He has to fuel the jet," her father answered. "You know, you remind me of your mother more and more every day." He reached up and touched her face. "I'm going to miss those cute freckles and that fiery red hair munchkin."

"Dad, I'm not your little girl anymore."

"I understand that you're an adult now sweetheart, but you will always be my little girl."

The divider between the driver and them lowered as the car came to a stop. "Do you need a ride back Ms. Smith?" the driver asked.

"No thanks Peter, I'll take the Porsche home. If I need you, I'll call."

"Alright. Have a safe trip sir."

"Thanks Peter," Malcolm said as he and Sara stepped out of the car. The limo drove away as Sara and Malcolm stood by the house that he bought when he won the lotto. It was nothing special, but he liked the location for the airport he built later.

As they walked toward the jet, a well-dressed man was jogging toward them. It was George, Malcolm's longtime assistant and his main pilot. "Sir, the plane's ready," he said.

Malcolm smiled softly. "Great! We're off!"

"Stay out of trouble little devil," George said. He had called Sara little devil ever since she was a little girl. Before being Malcolm's assistant and pilot, George was his best friend. He and Sara had always joked with each other.

"When are you going to stop calling me little devil?" Sara asked. "I'm not little anymore Georgie." George just smiled at her and turned for the plane.

"Your positive you don't want to go?" Malcolm asked again for reassurance.

"Dad, just go. I'll be fine."

"Alright," he said as he shook his head. "Man you are all grown up now aren't you?"

Sara rolled her eyes. "Have fun dad. I love you!"

"I love you too," he said as he hugged her. "See you soon sweetheart."

3

Malcolm walked toward the jet where George was waiting by the door. As they boarded George turned and waved. Sara waved back at him.

Some fear started to settle in Sara's stomach. She had never been left alone before. She wanted to learn how to live on her own but the thought was horrifying. She did not want her father to know though, because it would ruin his trip to Africa that he certainly deserved.

Sara watched as the plane began to roll down the runway. She listened to the jet's engine. She had always loved that sound. Except it sounded different this time. There was a louder rumble. She realized now that this sound was separate from the jet's engine. She looked into the sky to see a large ship coming toward the airport. It was like nothing she had ever seen. It sparkled in the sunlight. The ship was descending fast. Sara looked closer to see two fighter jets directly behind the large circular ship. Her father's jet had made it almost to the end of the runway now. Sara watched in horror. The fighter jets pulled up as the large ship continued to descend. Her father's jet lifted off the runway as the plummeting circular ship drew closer. Sara screamed as the two collided. "Daddy!" she wailed. The explosion was huge and totally destroyed the little jet. The larger ship was sliding down the runway now. It hardly looked damaged.

Sara was crying in disgust, "Why God? Why?" She hadn't felt this way since her mother had died. She knew that there was no chance her father or George had survived the explosion.

4

As the large ship came to rest on the runway, she looked up to see parachutes drifting down. She counted nine of them. Fear overtook her as she ran to the house and hid behind the porch swing. The men parachuting landed near each other by the runway, which was a good distance from her. They disconnected the parachutes and walked toward the immobilized ship with guns in hand. Now her sadness was temporarily transformed into fear and curiosity. The door to the large ship was slowly lowering like a drawbridge. The men out front looked on and pointed their guns toward the opening. Sara could hear one of them yelling orders.

"O'Dell, Rodriguez, go around the back to make sure none of them escape."

"Yes Captain," a large black man said. He and another man circled around to the back of the ship. Clearly Sara was about to see a war take place a few hundred feet from her. She wanted to stay hidden, but was too curious to go inside.

5

Suddenly, little gray men began to pour out of the door. There was about twenty of them and one was different from the rest. It was a little taller and had a green glow to it. Each creature had some type of gun in its hand.

The humans open fired. Some of the creatures started falling to the ground. The gray men fired back. Their guns seemed to shoot some kind of laser. The human's skin was disintegrating in large circular patterns around where the lasers hit them. Sara watched as a laser carved a eight inch circle through one of the soldier's chests. She could see through it the instant before his lifeless body fell to the ground. Each side was losing numbers. O'Dell and Rodriguez were circling back around now. The Captain got hit in the face and his head disintegrated. There were only two little gray men left and the glowing one. Only O'Dell and Rodriguez remained from the army side. Rodriguez shot one of the gray creatures in the head. It fell to the ground but did not seem to bleed. Despite the massacre there was no blood coming from any of the gray men. Sara noticed this now. O'Dell shot the other gray one. There was only the glowing green creature left now. His green flesh flashed bright, and the creature disappeared. Sara watched in awe. This was better than a David Blaine stunt. The creature reappeared behind Rodriguez, snapping his neck. O'Dell turned as the creature knocked his gun out of his hands. It shoved O'Dell to the ground. The creature approached the fallen soldier from a commanding position. O'Dell grabbed his knife from his belt and threw it, hitting the creature squarely in the throat. The green glow stopped as the creature fell to the ground. It also had no blood coming from its neck.

6

'What are these things?' Sara thought. *'Why don't they bleed?'* O'Dell got up. He picked up his gun and searched inside the ship for a few minutes and then came back out. Sara was unsure if she should approach the soldier. *'Why not? I have nothing left to lose.'* Sara stepped out from behind the porch swing and walked toward O'Dell. As she approached, O'Dell turned and noticed her. He quickly pointed his gun toward her.

"Don't shoot!" Sara cried.

"Identify yourself!" he yelled to her.

"I'm Sara Smith. This is my father's," she stopped herself. "This was my father's airport," she stated as she began to cry.

"I'm Michael O'Dell," the soldier declared as he lowered his gun. "You weren't supposed to see this. We tried to lure them to a secluded area."

"Well you fucked up and lured them right into my father's jet!" Sara yelled with anger. Tears were streaming down her face.

"I'm sorry," Michael stated as he walked up to her.

"What are they?" Sara asked as she wiped her cheek clean from tears.

"Aliens; this isn't the first time that they've come. My division is sent around to destroy them and cover up the mess. This time they were armed though."

"What do you mean this time?" Sara asked. "They weren't armed last time?"

"They have never been armed. They usually exit the ship with their hands in the air," O'Dell replied.

"Then what? You shoot them down like animals?"

"I just follow orders," O'Dell answered.

Sara shook her head in disagreement and walked over to the ship's wreckage. She picked up a panel off the side of the ship and held it in her hand. It was surprisingly light. She tried to bend it to no avail. The metal was extremely strong. "What kind of metal is this?" she asked O'Dell.

"I do not know. It is not from our world."

"You said that you were sent to clean up; what do you do with this metal?"

"Well, we haven't found a way to destroy it yet, so we have to bury it so others don't see it."

"Why?" Sara asked.

"Imagine the mass panic that it would cause if people knew that aliens existed; and that they had this type of technology."

"Or the anger they would have if they found out that their government was lying to them," she replied snidely.

7

Sara had an idea. She was interested in this metal. *'If these aliens could travel through space like this then why couldn't humans do the same. Besides, with my funding I could get the best team of people around to go with me.'*

"How do you bury a ship of this size?" she asked.

"I have to call my headquarters so they can send reinforcements," O'Dell stated.

"No!" Sara snapped. "This is my airport now. I will not have more troops snooping around."

"I'm sorry, but I must…."

"No!" she interrupted. "I'll pay you for the metal. That way you don't have to bury it."

"What?" Michael said confused. "It belongs to the US government."

"Name your price," she said confidently.

"It's not that easy. Like I said, it isn't mine to give," he replied.

"Sure it is. I want to rebuild this ship... and go into space."

"Your crazy! You can't do that. How do you know anything about space, or flight for that matter? How would you even know how to rebuild it?" he asked.

"I could get anyone I needed to help," she said. "In fact, I could use you Mike. Stay, be a part of my crew."

"I can't do that. I have obligations." He wasn't about to listen to this crazy girl. She could never accomplish this.

"Your obligations won't pay you a million dollars," she stated with a grin.

"Are you serious?" he asked.

"Yes," she laughed.

"A million dollars is no good if I die."

"I'll get the best crew I can get. In fact, you can pick who you need and I'll pay them."

Michael thought for a moment. *Sure she may be crazy, but she's also crazy rich. It might actually be possible.* His decision was made. "Okay, I'm in but we have to hurry. It usually takes us a week to bury the ship. If I don't report in a few days, the government will be very curious."

"Great, lets do it!" she said as she hugged him.

Chapter Two:
Recruiting

1

Sara and Michael talked about who else they could get for their mission into space. "A few years back I had to take a piece of this metal to a scientist named Thomas Simonson so he could examine it," O'Dell said. "If anyone knows what it takes to fly into space it's him."

"Great, where's he at?" Sara asked.

"He lives in Miami, near my brother, Jordan."

Sara remembered that a couple months earlier her father had to charter a few flights because his jet had broke down. She pulled out her phone.

"Who are you calling?" Michael asked.

"Wesley. He makes chartered flights for us when the jet is broke down. We will have to use him to get us where we need to go." Sara walked away from Michael as she began talking on the phone.

Michael watched her. *'Little spoiled red-head,'* he thought. *'Probably never worked a day in her life.'*

Sara returned to him. "Okay, Wesley will be here in about an hour."

"What? We're just going to fly down to Miami to see Professor Simonson?"

"Yeah, why not?" Sara replied with a smile.

2

The two of them went inside the house and waited for Wesley to arrive. They talked for about an hour when Sara saw a plane coming in. The little plane cleared the wreckage and landed on the runway.

"Come on," Sara said. "He's here." They went outside and walked over to the plane. Wesley was walking out of the plane as they approached. He was a skinny black man with braided hair.

"What the hell happened here!" he said referring to the wreckage. "You could have mentioned, 'Hey Wes watch out for the giant pile of destruction on the entrance of the runway'. I could have been killed," he said lightly.

Sara began to cry.

"What? I was only joking."

O'Dell leaned over and whispered in Wesley's ear. "That wreckage is her father's plane. He was in it."

"Oh no. I'm sorry girl," Wesley said as he went over and hugged her.

Sara cleared up her tears and introduced Wesley to Michael. She explained everything that had happened with the aliens. "We are going to use their ship to fly into space," she told him. "Do you want to be part of the team?"

"Hell yeah girl! You know I'm in for an adventure."

"Good, I will pay one million dollars to everyone that goes."

"Alright!" Wesley agreed. "I was just going for the fun of it but know I'm committed to working. So where to?"

"We need to get the rest of the team," Sara said. "First stop is Miami for Professor Simonson."

3

They flew to Miami and got a rental car. Wesley stayed with the plane while O'Dell and Sara went looking for Thomas Simonson.

"If you're really serious about this, can I go see my brother first?" O'Dell asked.

"Sure, but he can't know where we are going."

"I just want to say goodbye and get some clothes off him. I can't go back to my base for cloths without being spotted."

"Good idea," Sara said.

He pulled into a large house and they walked up the sidewalk. There was a doorbell but Michael knocked. Sara could hear footsteps coming toward the door from inside. A tall, thin black man opened the door.

"Hey Mike," he said. "You should visit more often. That doorbell's been fixed for three months now."

"You know I can't visit because of my job," O'Dell said.

"Yeah, I know. What brings you here," the man said as he shot an awkward glance at Sara.

"I need to borrow some clothes. I'm going away for awhile."

"Away? Does you're Captain know?"

"No, nobody can know. They are going to be looking for me and they can't know where I'm at; not that they could find me anyway."

"You're going AWOL?"

"Yeah, I guess I am."

"What'd you do? Knock up the white chick?" he asked as he looked at Sara.

"Excuse me," she said. "No."

"No Jordan, I just need to go. I'll be back. Can I borrow some clothes."

"Yeah I guess. That way you'll have to visit when you return them. You will return them, right?"

"Yes man. I don't have time for this. Can I just borrow some clothes."

"Sure, should've known you wouldn't have had time. Sorry for wanting to be a brother man."

"I promise you when I get back I'll have lots of time to spend with ya."

"What about moms. You visit her yet."

"I can't Jordan. I don't have time."

"Whatever dog. Take what you need."

Michael gathered a duffle bag and some of Jordan's clothes while Jordan went to the living room and ignored them. They left and went to the car.

"He's friendly," Sara said as they backed out of the driveway.

"It's my fault. I don't visit enough. I'm hoping that a million dollars will change that."

4

They drove for about twenty minutes and pulled up to a large blue house in a wealthy neighborhood.

"This is the address," Michael said. "This guy might be as rich as you, little girl?"

"I'm no little girl!" she yelled. "I'm twenty-one! Don't you forget whose funding this mission."

"Mission? This is no mission. This is damn near impossible. I'm just indulging you because I could use the money." He didn't believe that though. He believed it was possible. In fact, he was rather confident they could do it if they could convince Professor Simonson to come along.

"Well if it is the slightest bit possible, we are going to do it." She rang the doorbell to the enormous house. An older man answered the door. He must have been in his early fifties.

"May I help you?" the man asked.

"Professor Simonson, my name is Michael O'Dell. I brought you a piece of metal a few years back."

"You mustn't talk about that. No one is supposed to know!" he answered in an urgent soft voice.

"Yes, well… I was only following orders that day, but I'm afraid that I lied when I said that little piece of metal was all that survived the crash. The government wanted knowledge about the metal, but didn't want you to have access to the entire ship. In fact they didn't want you having access to enough metal to make a ship."

"Why for heavens sake not?" Simonson asked with anger on his face. "This could enhance our space travel. We could travel out of this solar system!"

"Exactly sir. They don't feel that we as a society are ready for that," Michael remarked.

"Who are they to slow science's progress?"

"They are the people in charge, that's who," O'Dell replied.

"Professor Simonson," Sara interjected, "my name is Sara Smith. I intend to change all that. I have access to an entire ship. If we could repair it, then we could travel wherever you wanted to go."

"Things like this cost money my dear."

"Money is no object. I just need you to be a part of the expedition. I will pay you generously."

"My darling," he said with a chuckle as he pushed his glasses up on his large round nose, "I don't need your money. But if you're willing to fund this so-called expedition, count me in."

"Great," Sara said as she smiled. "We start immediately."

"Yes we must act quickly," Michael added.

"I can't do all the repairs by myself though. Can I bring Coy, my mechanic?"

"As long as we keep this top secret. Will he be willing to go?"

"Give him the money that was intended for me. If you offer him money, he'll go. He could certainly use the money more than I could."

"Sounds good," Sara said.

The professor quickly packed some necessities and followed them to the car. Sara drove with Simonson in the front seat giving her directions to Coy's house. Michael sat in the back. Tom Petty was playing on the radio. The song was called 'Running Down A Dream'. *'How fitting,'* Simonson thought.

5

They drove for about twenty minutes until they reached Coy's neighborhood. The houses on the side of the road looked different now. They were a lot smaller and there was trash in the yards. A few dirty kids ran up the broken sidewalk.

"This is it," Simonson said as he pointed to a small, ranch-style home. Sara pulled into the driveway behind a jacked up car. There was an old pick-up truck parked in the yard next to another car that was up on blocks. They all got out of the car and approached the front door. Right before they got to the doorstep, the door opened. A tall muscular blonde man came out.

"Professor. Wow, what brings you here?" he asked.

"Coy, I want you to meet some new friends of mine. This is Michael O'Dell and Sara Smith."

"I'm Coy Riggs. How do you do?" Coy said as he shook their hands. "Come on in," he said as they all entered the living room. "Don't mind the mess. I wasn't expecting company. Have a seat," he said as he motioned toward the couch. The three of them sat on the couch while Coy sat across from them in a chair. "How can I help you?"

Sara explained what happened and how they were going to fix the ship and needed his help.

"Gosh that is all very interesting. I'm not familiar with fixing spaceships though. I just fix cars. I'm not sure I'd be much help."

"No one is experienced at fixing alien spacecraft," Simonson said. "I'm sure I can figure out the basics though, I just need you to do the dirty work."

"Okay, I guess I could help you all," Coy responded.

"We want you to go with us also," Sara said. "In case the ship breaks down."

"Boy, I don't know," Coy answered.

"I'll pay you a million dollars," Sara added.

"Holy smokes!" Coy shouted. " Sounds like a deal." Coy packed some of his things and went with them back to the plane.

6

They all boarded the plane to see Wesley sleeping on the floor.

"Hey Wes!" Sara shouted. He sat up startled.

"Damn girl you done scared the hell out of me."

"What are you doing sleeping on the floor?" she asked.

"It makes my back feel better," he responded as he glanced over at Coy and Simonson. "They in on it?" he asked.

"Yes, this is Coy Riggs and Professor Thomas Simonson."

"How the hell are you," Wesley shouted. "I'm Wesley Sparks; your pilot on this mad adventure." He walked over to them. "Nice to meet you Professor," he said as he shook Coy's hand joking.

"No I'm Coy," he said not comprehending that Wesley was picking on him.

"Sure you are," he said as he walked up front. "Where to sweet cheeks."

"Give it up Wes," Sara said. "Let's go back to my airport."

"You got it."

They all relaxed as the plane took off and headed back North. On the way back everyone was talking and getting acquainted. "Professor," Sara said. "Do you really think that it is possible?"

"Sweetie, if this ship of yours exists, anything is possible. We will need a few more people and supplies though."

"Well what do we need?" she asked.

"It would be good to have a biologist, botanist, and geologist with us. We could also use a journalist to document everything."

"How about a chef?" Coy added.

"A chef?" Wesley interjected from up front. "You're like six foot four dude, you don't need to grow anymore."

"Wes, be nice," Sara said. "We'll see about the chef Coy."

7

They arrived back at the crash site just before dusk. After the plane landed, everyone exited and walked over to the spaceship that was still well intact. "Good lord!" Simonson said with interest. "This is marvelous! It seems to be in great shape. Can you fix the damage to the outside Coy?"

"It looks quite easy to fix. I just need the right tools and supplies."

"How much money do you need to get them?" Sara asked.

"Gee, I don't know,"

"I'll write you a check for five thousand. Will that cover it?" she asked.

"Yeah, but how am I going to get the tools?" Coy asked.

Sara reached into the tight front pocket of her jeans and pulled out a set of keys and tossed them to O'Dell. "You and Michael can take the Porsche tomorrow while the Professor, Wesley and I find more people for the expedition."

"Wait," Wesley said. "Maybe I want to take the Porsche. Let G.I. Joe here fly the damn plane."

Sara ignored Wes, which is the only way to put up with his constant joking and picking.

Simonson went into the ship and inspected its navigational panel. He was amazed by the technology, but surprised by its simplicity. *'I think a twelve year old could fly this thing,'* he thought. After a short while, they all went inside the house and settled down for the night. The professor took one of the bedrooms, while Sara had the other. Michael had the couch, while Wes and Coy slept on the floor.

8

Early the next morning Sara was making pancakes. The smell of smoke had awoken everyone except Wesley who was still sound asleep on the floor.

"I'm sorry," Sara said. "I don't have a lot of experience cooking.

"See we could use a chef," Coy said. "No offence though. I mean, you tried and that was sweet." Sara smiled and walked into the living room where Wes was still sound asleep on his back. She quietly knelt beside him and screamed "Wake up!!!!"

Wesley snapped up startled. "What the...damn you. You could have given me a heart attack."

"Time is wasting. We need to get around and get going," she said.

"It would have been nice if you were laying here next to me," Wes said with a grin.

"If that ever happens, then you do need to get up because you're dreaming," she replied.

They all got around and grabbed some cereal, except for Coy. He ate the burnt pancakes.

It was still early morning when they headed outside.

"Do your best on the ship," Sara said to Coy. "I don't know when we'll be back. It may be a couple days."

Wesley went in and prepped the plane while Sara and Professor Simonson talked. "So do you know any biologists, botanists, or geologists?" she asked.

"I know a geologist that would love to go. His name is Paul Finch. He lives in Houston and is a good friend of mine. He and I have always talked about space and other planets."

"Great!" Sara said. "What about a biologist or botanist?"

"A botanist, no. But I know a biologist that is superb. She is in Kenya right now."

Sara began to cry. "My father should be in Kenya right now too. I have nothing left here. My life is a wreck. I have never done anything to be proud of. That is why I'm doing this. I'm doing this for my father: to make him proud."

"Sara darling, from the looks of things your father had a lot of reasons to be proud of you."

"Thanks Professor. Lets head to Houston to see Mr. Finch." They boarded the plane and told Wesley the plan.

9

Michael and Coy began making a list of supplies as they watched the plane fly away. After they finished the list, they began walking toward the Porsche.

"This is going to be fun huh?" Michael said.

"Do you mean the Porsche or the spaceship?" Coy asked.

"The Porsche silly. Do you think fixing the spaceship is going to be fun?"

"Well, I'll enjoy it. I like solving problems, but I'm not really too smart you know. So, I enjoy fixing things because it's the one thing I am good at."

"Don't sell yourself short my friend. I'm sure there are several things you do well," Michael said.

"Well I can certainly make pancakes better than Sara," he said as they both laughed. Michael and Coy got in the shiny silver Porsche. Coy slid his seat back as far as it would go just to allow his legs to fit. "This is going to be a fun ride isn't it?" Coy said.

"Coy, you fix that space ship and that will be one hell of a fun ride."

Chapter Three:
Reunions

1

When they arrived in Houston, Wesley stayed with the plane while Sara and Professor Simonson rented a car. The professor drove a couple miles until they reached a rather nice neighborhood. They pulled into a nice two-story house and got out. They walked up to the front door and the professor rang the doorbell. A man in his late forties answered the door.

"Tom," the man said as they shook hands. "What brings you here and who is this lovely companion of yours?"

"This is my friend Sara Smith."

"Nice to meet you," Paul said as he shook her hand.

"Mr. Finch," Sara said. "We are here to invite you on an adventure with us."

"Well that sounds interesting. What kind of an adventure?"

"We have a ship," Simonson said with glee. "We are going into space."

"Ooh a NASA mission," Paul said excited.

"No, not exactly," Tom answered. "More like a Sara Smith mission."

"I'm willing to pay you a million dollars if you go with us," Sara added.

"Well count me in! Let me pack my things,"

"Quickly Mr. Finch," Sara said.

2

They all went back to the plane where Wesley was again sleeping. "What is wrong with you?" Sara asked. "Is that all you do is sleep?"

"Hey, I need my beauty sleep baby. So I can look good for you."

"In order to look good for me you'll need a beauty coma."

"Ouch, that's harsh girl," he replied.

They introduced Wesley to Mr. Finch as the plane headed for Kenya.

"So this biologist; she's really good?" Sara asked.

"She is the best," Simonson answered. "I love her like a daughter."

"Is this Michelle you're talking about?" Paul asked.

"Yes," Simonson answered. "I can't wait to see her. It has been so long"

"Have you met her Mr. Finch?" Sara asked.

"No. Tom has told me all about her though."

"How do you know her Professor?" Sara asked him.

"Her parents and I were very close friends and I love what she does for animals so I usually help fund her programs."

"What does she do in Kenya, Professor?"

"She does Safari tours to help fund her true cause; helping cheetah and leopard populations. She started a captive breeding program for cheetahs, leopards, and caracals. Last I heard, she wanted to help rhinos as well but didn't have the funding yet."

"What the hell is a caracal?" Wesley yelled from up front.

"It's another wild cat in Kenya," Simonson said. "Michelle loves the cat family."

"Do you think she will go with us?" Sara asked.

"She is caught up in her work, but I think if you offer her what you offered the others she would gladly go. She's not at all selfish, but this would help her tremendously."

"Where in Kenya are we headed?" Wesley asked.

"Narok," Tom said. "Michelle lives in Narok."

"Where is that? Is that near Nairobi or Mombasa?"

"It is about a hundred kilometers west of Nairobi. It is between Nairobi and the Masai Mara Wildlife Reserve."

"Oh," Wesley said.

"Can you land in a field?" Professor Simonson asked.

"Dude, I can land anywhere you want. I'm that damn good."

"Alright then," Simonson said as he turned back to Sara and Paul with wide eyes. Sara chuckled a little.

3

It was still morning in Kenya when they landed in a small field outside of Narok. As usual, Wesley stayed with the plane as Sara, Tom and Paul walked into town to get Michelle.

As they entered town, the streets were lined with souvenir shops. There were various artifacts and shields from the Masai people. Occasionally they would walk past one of the tall, thin, Masai standing on the street in their red tribal garb. They arrived at a little building and walked up the stairs to a second story apartment. The professor knocked on the door.

"Nani?" a female voice from inside said.

"Michelle this is Tom. Speak English, I can't understand Swahili," he said as he laughed. The door flung open and a young, beautiful blonde swung her arms around Professor Simonson.

"Oh Tom, I missed you!"

"I missed you too darling," he answered. "Michelle, this is Paul Finch and Sara Smith."

"Michelle Austin," she said as she shook their hands. There was a large cheerful smile on her face.

"Sara has invited us all on an adventure and we want you to be a part of it," Tom said.

"Actually we need you to be a part of it," Sara added.

"Boy, I'm not sure. I'm so busy here with the Captive Breeding Program,"

"Wait until you here the details before you make your decision," Tom said.

"Well we shouldn't divulge our plan unless we know that she is in due to the secrecy that is needed," Sara explained. "Let me just put it this way. There will be a check in your name for a million dollars if you decide to go with us."

"Sure," Michelle said with doubt.

"Oh she's quite serious darling," Simonson said.

"Oh my god. Do you realize how much this will help my program! How long will we be gone?"

"We don't know," Simonson said.

"Where are we going?" she asked.

"I take it that you are on board now?" Sara asked her.

"Yeah, I mean a million dollars! I'd fly to the moon for that."

Tom and Sara exchanged smiles at her comment.

"How about farther?" Finch said as they chuckled. Michelle looked confused.

"Oh he's quite serious darling," Tom said as they all laughed.

"I'm in! When do we leave?"

"We leave here today."

"Oh my god," Michelle said. "Let me call Joseph to see if he can handle the program while I'm gone."

"Sure," Sara said.

Michelle picked up the phone and dialed. Sara listened to Michelle but didn't understand because she was talking in Swahili.

"Jambo," Michelle said. "Mzuri sana na wewe?"

Michelle began to pack as they talked on the phone. The conversation was ending as she walked out of the bedroom. "Leo," Michelle continued in Swahili. "Sijui………..Ndiyo……………Hakuna matata…………Mzuri………….Sawa sawa, Kwaheri."

"You didn't say anything about the mission did you?" Sara asked.

"No." Michelle said with a smile. "I just asked him if he could handle the program for awhile because I was going away."

"That was Swahili that you were speaking in?" Sara asked her.

"Yeah, why?"

"I could've sworn I heard hakuna matada in there. You know from The Lion King."

"You did. Apparently Timon and Pumba speak Swahili too," Michelle said with a smile.

"So do I then," Sara said as she giggled. "It means no worries."

"No problem, no worries, same thing," Michelle said. "OK. I'm ready."

They began to walk back to the plane. "How many people are going with us?" Michelle asked.

"Well, there's two back at the site, one on the plane, and the four of us." Tom said.

"We still need to find a botanist and a journalist," Sara added.

"A botanist?" Michelle asked. "My roommate in college was a botanist."

"Do you think she would want to go?" Sara asked.

"She is doing cancer research down in Brazil right now, but if she was offered the same as me, she would definitely go."

Sara wiped a tear from her eye. The irony was surprising. Michelle was in Kenya where her father was supposed to be going and now a botanist that is studying cures for cancer, a disease that left her without a mother. "Do you know where in Brazil?" Sara asked her.

"Yes, I can show you," Michelle answered.

They all boarded the plane where Wesley was actually awake. "How do you do," he said to Michelle as he extended his hand. "I'm Wesley Sparks, your pilot today; and any other day you want."

Michelle smiled as she shook his hand. "Michelle Austin; your biologist," she stated.

"I've always wanted my own biologist," Wesley said. "Can I keep her?"

"Down boy," Sara replied.

"Where to?" Wesley asked.

"Brazil," Sara answered as they began to take off.

4

Back at the crash site, Coy and Michael had returned with the supplies and were almost finished with the repairs.

"Do you think this is going to be dangerous?" Coy asked. "I mean I can fix the ship so it is like brand new, but that doesn't mean we won't have problems."

"Coy, all you have to worry about is your part, my friend. Sara is assembling the best crew to get us through this safely, but it is still going to be dangerous. Who knows what we will encounter out there."

"There, I'm done," Coy said.

"Will it fly?" O'Dell asked.

"If it flew before, it should fly now."

5

On the plane everyone was talking about Michelle's botanist friend.

"What is her name," Sara asked.

"Tabitha Jones," Michelle answered.

"Another chick," Wesley yelled from up front. "I like it."

"Calm your hormones," Sara said.

"Where am I going in Brazil?" Wesley asked.

"Her lab is in Manaus," Michelle replied.

"It will be night when we arrive," Tom said. "We should catch some zzzzz's and get Tabitha in the morning."

"Good idea Professor," Sara added.

6

Back at the site, Coy and Michael had finished their work and went inside. Coy sat on the couch as Michael went over to the liquor cabinet. "Hey Coy, she's got some good stuff in here."

"Do you really think we should touch that without her permission?"

"You need to lighten up man. She's a millionaire. She's not going to care if we have some vodka." Michael opened a bottle of vodka and went to the kitchen. "You going to celebrate with me or what?" he asked Coy.

"I guess we might as well," Coy said.

Michael returned with two glasses and began to pour the vodka.

7

As the plane landed at the Eduardo Gomes International Airport in Manaus nightfall had overcome the skies. "Do you guys want me to get a hotel?" Sara asked.

"I'm all for staying on the plane," Tom said.

"It would be quicker," Finch agreed.

"Is anyone against staying on the plane?" Sara asked. She looked around to see a very cooperative group of people. No one disagreed with the idea. Everyone made due and crowded on the floor of the plane except Simonson and Finch who preferred the upright seats.

"Hey Sara," Wes whispered. "You're laying next to me yet, I'm not dreaming." Sara just rolled her eyes. "Wanna cuddle?" Wesley said to her with a smile.

"Wes, get the picture. It will never happen. Lying on the same floor is as close as you'll ever get."

8

Meanwhile, Coy and Michael were both highly intoxicated and loving every minute of it. "Hey Mike, we're rich!" Coy said as he began laughing.

"Yes we are. I'll probably need every penny once I get thrown out of the military for this."

"You can come live in my new mansion," Coy laughed.

"I'll have one of my own man."

"When do you think Sara and the professor will return?" Coy asked.

"Not tonight. Drink up!" O'Dell said as he downed the vodka left in his cup.

"Do you think we'll die?" Coy asked.

"For drinking?"

"No," Coy laughed. "We're going into space."

"Oh yeah that. We might." They both broke out in hysterical laughter.

9

Morning had arrived in Manaus. Paul decided to stay at the plane with Wesley. Tom, Sara, and Michelle left the plane and rented a car. They traveled west until they reached a small lab. They got out and walked up to the door. They all peered through the door to see a young black woman working hard. Michelle opened the door and crept inside.

"Hi Tabby," she said softly.

"Shelly!" she cheered. "What are you doing here?" Tabby was the only person who had ever referred to Michelle as Shelly. She said that it sounded more fun and playful than Michelle. This was the first time they had seen each other in almost a year.

"I came with some friends of mine," Michelle answered as Tom and Sara slowly walked in behind her.

"Is this the Tom that I've heard so much about?" Tabitha asked as she shook his hand.

"Yes," Michelle answered. "And this is Sara Smith."

"Hi, I'm Tabitha Jones. You can call me Tabby." They shook hands and everyone followed Tabby into a small break room for the lab.

"I'll keep this brief," Sara said. "We want you to go with us on a mission. You will need to leave today. I will pay you a million dollars."

Tabitha's eyes grew large as she looked over to Michelle in disbelief. "Is she for real?" Tabby asked.

"I've been offered the same amount," Michelle said. "Why else would I leave my cats?"

"I'm in. I have to go home and pack though."

"Michelle can go with you," Sara said. "Meet us back at the plane Michelle. You can fill her in on the way. Please hurry."

"Okay," Michelle agreed.

Sara and Tom joined Paul and Wesley back at the plane.

"Where's goldilocks?" Wesley asked.

"She is helping Ms. Tabitha Jones pack," Sara answered.

Wesley smiled at the thought of another female joining the team.

10

Back at the site, Coy and Michael were just waking up. Coy had slept on the floor and Michael was face down on the coffee table. "That was fun huh Mike,"

"Owe… yeah. Remind me not to try to out drink you again." They took turns in the shower and relaxed around the house for the day.

Michelle and Tabitha had returned to the plane. Sara introduced Tabitha to Paul and Wesley, who was all smiles.

"Where to Sara?" Wes asked.

"Back to NY. Hopefully Coy and Michael are finished with the ship."

"That is high hopes," Wes said. "I would just hope that your Porsche is in one piece."

They flew back to the Allison Smith Memorial Airport and landed just before dark. Paul was amazed at the scene that lay out in front of him. "What an amazing ship," he said. Michael and Coy walked outside to greet everyone as they exited the plane. Everyone was introduced and went inside to get to know each other.

"So Tabitha, how old are you," Wesley asked. "If you don't mind me asking."

"I'm twenty-seven, how 'bout you?"

"I'm the ripe age of thirty," he answered. "How about everyone else?" Wes asked.

"I just turned twenty-one," Sara stated.

"Twenty-eight," Michelle said. O'Dell mentioned that he was thirty-six.

"I'm thirty-three," Coy said.

"Paul and I plead the fifth," Simonson said with a chuckle.

"So was everything fixable," Sara asked Coy.

"It appears to be in good shape," he answered. "I don't know what kind of mileage this thing gets but it appears to have plenty of fuel left also."

"So what's the plan?" O'Dell asked Sara.

"The girls and I will drive into the Big Apple tomorrow and look for a chef and a journalist. By tomorrow night, we should leave."

"Sounds good," Tom said.

"A chef?" Wesley questioned. "You're seriously getting a chef just because the too-tall toe head here wants one. Maybe I want a stripper."

"Well, I would get one of those but I don't think the rest of the guys would want to see him strip."

"Very funny sweet cheeks. Just go get your damn chef tomorrow." Wesley was shaking his head.

They all made room and found a place to sleep for the night.

Chapter Four:
Trip To The City

1

The next morning the girls piled into the Porsche and headed for New York City. Sara and Michelle were in front while Tabby leaned forward from the back. Her hands grabbed the top of each seat as they all chatted.

At the house, the men were taking turns with the bathroom. Coy and Simonson were talking while waiting for Wesley to finish his shower.

"Professor, where are we going to fly this ship to?" Coy asked.

"Well our next closest star is Alpha Centauri. It has a planet at the perfect distance to support life. I do not know however if its atmosphere has poisonous gasses or oxygen. I guess we will have to see."

"That sounds comforting," O'Dell said as he approached them. "Will we have enough fuel to get us there?"

"I'm not sure," Simonson said. "We should. The creatures that brought the ship made it here and they barely used any of the fuel in the fuel cell."

"Are we going to be able to find this planet?" Coy asked.

"From what I saw when I entered the ship the navigational system was amazing Coy," Tom said with a smile. "I won't really know if we will fully understand it until we actually fire it up. I don't understand the language on the control panel, but there are diagrams. I think we can figure it out."

2

The girls reached the city by eleven. They decided to stop for lunch. They sat down and chatted while waiting for their food to arrive. It was a modest restaurant with reasonable prices.

"You know, any chef would do for our expedition," Sara said.

"I don't even think we need a chef," Michelle added.

"I know, but I figured I'd get one for Coy's sake and to tick Wesley off."

The girls laughed lightly over this as their food was delivered.

When they finished their meals, Sara asked the waiter if they could meet the chef. He hesitated at first until he saw the extremely generous tip sitting under the napkin dispenser. He led them back into the kitchen where a middle-aged man with black hair was cooking over a stove. "Steve, these women wanted to meet you," the waiter said.

"Well, must be my lucky day," the chef said. "Was my food that good?"

"Good enough," Sara answered. "We want you to come with us."

Steve smiled. "Three lovely ladies want to take me with them. I can't resist that. When and where?"

Sara walked up to him and grabbed his hand. "On an adventure, right now," she said.

"Right now? I can't leave work."

"I'll pay you one million dollars," Sara added.

"Is this for real?" he asked as he looked over to Michelle and Tabitha.

"Yes it's for real," Michelle said. "Come outside and talk to us."

"I take it love is not what you three are looking for."

Sara laughed, "No, just a chef, but I'll pay a million dollars for your services."

"How do I know you're telling the truth?" Steve said.

"Tell you what, I'll sleep with you if I'm lying," Sara said.

"No offence, but I don't think that having sex with you is an even trade for a million dollars," Steve said.

"Isn't it worth finding out now though?" Sara asked "Either way you win. And trust me sweetie, sex with me is worth more than a million dollars."

"Okay, I'll go with you guys," Steve said.

As they walked through the restaurant the waiter gave them a startled look. "Tell Joe that I quit," Steve said.

"What?" the waiter replied startled as they walked out.

"Nice ride," Steve said as he hopped into the back of the Porsche with Tabby. He directed them about six blocks to his apartment where they let him out to pack. He came back a few minutes later and hopped in.

3

They continued down the street until they saw Madison Square Gardens. The sign outside stated: Woman's ISKA Kickboxing Championship.

"Lets go watch that," Sara said. "We will get our journalist in there." She parked the car and they entered MSG. They approached the ticket booth. "I need ringside seats," Sara stated.

"I only have two left," The lady behind the desk said.

"I'll take them," Sara replied. "Tabby, do you remember how to get back to the airport?"

"Yeah, why?"

Sara reached into her pocket and pulled out her checkbook. She wrote a check out to Tabby for five thousand dollars and handed it to her. "I need you guys to get us supplies," Sara said. "We need lots of canned goods, and water, and whatever else you can think of."

"All that stuff isn't going to fit in the Porsche," Steve commented.

"So rent a truck or something," Sara said. "We'll meet back at the airport tonight. You can fill Steve in on the way."

"Okay," Tabby agreed. Steve and Tabby left while Sara and Michelle went to get their seats.

4

As they sat down the ring announcer welcomed everyone. "Welcome to the quarter finals of the ISKA Woman's Full Contact Kickboxing Championship. There are just eight women left competing for the title of the toughest woman in the world."

Sara glanced over to her left to see a man writing in a notebook. "Excuse me," she said. "May I ask what you are doing?"

"I'm writing notes," the man said, "for my paper."

"You're a reporter?" she asked.

"Well, yes."

"Why aren't you up in the press box with all the other journalists?"

"I'm afraid my paper isn't known well enough to get those kinds of credentials," he answered. "I'm William Day, I own the Day Times."

"Catchy," Sara said as she laughed. "I'm Sara Smith and this is my friend Michelle Austin. I have the story of a lifetime for you Mr. Day, and I'll pay you a million dollars to write it."

"Yeah, if it were only that easy," he said.

"Oh but it is," Sara replied.

"She's telling the truth," Michelle added.

"You have to travel with us though," Sara mentioned.

"I'll do it, but after the championship," he answered. Sara agreed.

"So," Michelle asked, "Who are the favorites here?"

"Katarina Kova from Russia, Li Wu from China, and Jade Evans from the U.S." he replied.

5

The ring announcer entered the ring again and began to announce the first two fighters. "Making her way down to the ring, fighting out of the blue corner from Dijon, France; Monique Mokai. And her opponent fighting out of the red corner from Krakow, Poland, Susan Horowitz. The referee for this bout is Hideki Tanaka."

The bell rang and the fight began. Horowitz was a big girl; six foot tall and well built. Mokai was faster and more agile though. There were a few punches from both fighters that didn't connect well. Then, Mokai executed a flying spin kick that caught Horowitz on the nose. Blood squirted out. Down she went. Despite Horowitz's size she was no match for Mokai. The level of violence was shocking for Sara and Michelle who glanced at each other after the first fight. William was still writing away.

The next fight was between Heidi Swartz from Oldenburg, Germany, and Katarina Kova from Moscow, Russia. Kova was the biggest woman Sara had ever seen. She must have been over six and a half feet tall. Swartz attacked first getting in three ineffective kicks before Kova drove her fist into Swartz's face dropping her instantly. One punch is all it took. Sara thought Swartz was dead. It took several minutes for Swartz to get up.

The next match had Li Wu from Kunming, China against Elsa Monitez from Aragon, Spain. Li Wu was only about five and a half feet tall. Monitez was at least four or five inches taller. Li Wu was the aggressor. She started with about six quick punches to the ribs and a kick to the face. Then she did a roundhouse kick that lifted

Monitez off the ground. Down she went. Sara had never seen someone move as fast as Li Wu did.

The last quarterfinal match was between Jade Evans, of Cheshire, NY and Zati Mabika from Jos, Nigeria. This looked like it was going to be a good match. Both fighters were about five foot ten. Mabika started the fight with a right-handed swing. Evans dodged left and punched Mabika in the face. Mabika countered with a high kick, but Evans dropped to the mat and swept Mabika's leg. Mabika hit the mat hard, but quickly flipped up onto her feet. Mabika went for a jumping roundhouse. Evans jumped at the same time and landed her foot on Mabika's chest, dropping her again. Mabika stayed down this time.

6

Sara glanced to her left to see William still writing away. He was a blonde haired man in his early thirties. After a slight pause, the fighting continued. There were four fighters left now as the Semifinals started. First up, Katarina Kova against Monique Mokai. Mokai attacked the gigantic Kova with a series of kicks that had seemingly no effect. Then punches to the face followed by a roundhouse that made Kova stumble backwards. Kova regained her poise and placed her left hand on the back of Mokai's head and punched with her right. Blood sprayed into the air as Mokai dropped motionless to the mat. Paramedics rushed to her side and hauled her off on a stretcher.

The next match was between the super fast Li Wu and well-rounded Jade Evans. Wu fiercely attacked with an onslaught of punches. All of them blocked except the last punch that connected with Evans's chin, jarring her head back. Evans retaliated with two punches to the ribs. Then, she jumped into the air and spun, kicking Li Wu in the face. Her left foot hit first followed by her right as she continued to spin. Evans landed gracefully on her feet as Wu fell to the mat.

Sara glanced over to see William writing away with a smile on his face. She looked to her right at Michelle who was clearly enjoying herself. "This is pretty neat huh?" Sara said.

"Yes, thank you," Michelle replied. "I like Jade Evans, I want her to win."

"Me too," Sara said. "I'm not sure she has a chance against that giant though."

Michelle just smiled in agreement. The fighters had now made their way to the ring for the championship bout, Katarina Kova versus Jade Evans. The bell rang and the fight began. Kova swung and missed. Evans countered with a kick to Kova's left leg. Kova swung again as Evans dodged and kicked her leg again. This continued on for minutes, Evans hopping around gracefully while dodging and countering with leg kicks. Kova began to wobble. Her leg was clearly bothering her. Then, Evans jumped up and spun, kicking Kova in the head with her left foot followed by her right foot. Evans landed gracefully as Kova dropped like a tall tree that had just been cut. Nobody yelled 'timber' but everyone in the arena knew the tree was falling. Jade Evans was the ISKA Women's Kickboxing Champion.

Sara looked over at Michelle, "I want her as a part of our team." William had finished writing now. "Where are the locker rooms?" Sara asked the reporter.

"Why? They won't let you in. I have tried to meet Jade Evans so many times and have never succeeded."

"I'll get in," Sara said bluntly.

7

William led them to the locker rooms where a large security guard stood ground. Sara handed the large man a nice wad of cash. "May I please go in? I'm not a reporter or a crazed fan I just need to talk to Jade Evans personally."

"I never saw you," he said as he stepped aside to let them by. Michelle and Sara walked through the entrance as the security guard stopped William. "I remember you. You're that crazy guy who keeps trying to see Ms. Evans. I can't let you in you'll have to stay here."

"I'm not crazy. I'm just a big fan." William said as he shook his head. He sat on a bench and waited for the girls to return.

Jade was the only person in the locker room when Sara and Michelle walked in. She was gathering several duffle bags that all seemed full. "How did you get in here?" Jade asked.

"It's amazing what you can do when you have money," Sara said.

"What do you want?" Jade asked impatiently.

"I'm Sara Smith and this is Michelle Austin. We want you to go on an adventure with us."

Jade laughed, "Yeah, that's going to happen." She started to grab her things.

"I'll pay you one million dollars," Sara added.

"Not interested," Jade emphasized as she began to walk away.

Sara and Michelle followed her. "You're not interested in a million dollars?" Michelle asked.

"Nobody buys me," Jade said.

Sara was still struggling for the reason Jade turned her down. "Is it because of your family?"

"I have no family," Jade answered coldly.

"Jade, just give us a moment, please," Sara pleaded.

"Alright, fine. You want to know why I don't want to go with you? First tell me why you want me to go with you."

"I watched you fight today and it was very inspirational," Sara said. "It made me want to know you."

"Plus we could use your protection," Michelle added.

"I don't want to go, because I'm not good with people," Jade answered.

"We can change that," Sara said with a bright smile. "Please!"

Jade paused and thought for a moment. "Alright," she agreed.

"Yes!" Sara cheered as Michelle smiled.

"How long will we be gone?" Jade asked.

"We're not sure," Michelle said.

"Well where are we going?" Jade asked.

"We're not sure," Sara answered.

"What do you know?" Jade asked with a smile.

"We are actually going to go into space," Sara said.

"Are you kidding? How did you manage that one?"

"We have a ship," Michelle said. "You in?"

"Sure," Jade said.

"Do you need to go anywhere to get any more clothes?" Sara asked.

"No, I've been here for a couple weeks. I have everything I need in these bags. I could use a hand with the bags though."

Michelle and Sara each grabbed a bag as they walked out of the locker room. William was still outside on a bench. He eagerly walked over to them. "Hey Jade, can I ask you a few questions?"

"No, I hate reporters," she said coldly. He continued to walk next to her as Jade looked over to Sara. "He's not going with us is he?"

"Yes," Sara said. "We need a journalist to document our accomplishments. Jade this is William Day."

"Don't write anything about me! Got it?" Jade said.

"I'll have to include you," William said. "Where are we going? You haven't even told me what we are doing." Everyone got into the Porsche and William pointed the way to his apartment so he could pack. William shared the back seat with Jade. He was intently staring at her. He watched as a bead of sweat rolled slowly down her forehead to the rim of her eyebrow. He reached over and wiped it off her head.

"Back off!" Jade yelled. "What the hell is wrong with you?"

"I didn't want it to get in your eye. That would sting," he explained.

"It would also sting if I kicked your ass." They arrived at William's apartment. Jade stayed in the car as everyone else went upstairs. While there Sara and Michelle filled him in.

8

Back at the airport, Steve and Tabby had arrived with a large U-Haul full of supplies. Michael, Coy, and Wesley helped them transfer them to the ship. Steve was introduced to everyone as they prepared for tomorrows lift off. Later that night, Sara returned with Michelle, Jade, and William. They too were introduced to the rest of the team.

"Where did you get this ship from?" William asked.

"I got it from the aliens that landed it here," Sara said with a smile.

"This really is a great story. We are going to fly this?"

"We are going to try," she answered.

Everyone gathered inside and sat down to eat their last supper on Earth for a while. Steve had made a simple spaghetti supper for everyone.

"Now this is what I'm talking about," Coy said. "This is good cooking."

"So Jade," William said. "Why do you fight?"

"Are you kidding me," she answered. "I told you no questions."

"I'm just trying to create conversation."

"No," she said. "You're just trying to get a story."

"Damn, she's a feisty one," Wesley said. "I better stay away from her."

"Plus she could kick your ass," Sara added. "She's the number one female kickboxer in the world."

"I was hoping you took me up on that stripper idea," Wesley said.

9

After supper, Sara called them all to the living room for a meeting. "Tomorrow we will embark on a great mission," she said as she stood in front of them. "We will attempt to fly into space, and beyond our solar system. I have assembled all of you for a reason. You each play an intricate part in this expedition. I have Tom Simonson, our scientist who will navigate us to a safe destination. Coy Riggs will keep everything running properly. Paul Finch our Geologist will study whatever rocks we find at this new destination. We can only hope we get to use the expertise of Tabitha Jones our Botanist and Michelle Austin our Biologist. They are here in case we encounter life, which I now know exists out there. Michael O'Dell and Jade Evans will provide protection for us. Steve Hanson is our chef who will provide our meals. Wesley Sparks is simply along for entertainment purposes." Everyone chuckled as Wesley shook his head. "Actually Wesley will be helping Professor Simonson fly the ship. We've got a good crew and we're going to do something spectacular tomorrow. We are leaving early in the morning after breakfast. Have a good night everyone."

Everyone made due and found places to sleep. Sara, O'Dell and Simonson stayed up for awhile and went over the details of the mission. Finally at about 12:30 they went to sleep.

Chapter Five:
Lift Off

1

The next morning everyone took turns in the shower. This took longer than expected. Sara was making a phone call to Peter her limo driver. "Peter, this is Sara. I'm going on vacation for a long time and I need you to handle my affairs. Get with Sylvia our accountant and tell her you'll be handling my accounts. She will ask you for a password. The password is *little devil*. I can't tell you any more. Bye."

Simonson was in the final stages of preparing the ship. Coy, Michael, Paul, and Wesley were helping him. Sara approached them. "Do we have enough supplies?" she asked.

"Good lord," Simonson said. Those two brought back the whole damn store. We have plenty of food and water."

"Sara," O'Dell said. "Come see what Coy and I did." Sara entered the ship with him to the large chamber. Inside were ten cots made out of wood. They had new twin-sized mattresses on each of them. "I would have made eleven if I knew you were bringing Jade."

"That's okay. One of us will have to be up at all times anyway," she said.

Everyone boarded the ship and gathered in the control center. Professor Simonson started the ship up. There was a light rumble at first, but it was surprisingly quiet. Michael and Wesley sat next to him.

"As soon as we're airborne, the government will have fighter jets after us," O'Dell explained.

"I know," Simonson said. "That is when I hit this." He pointed to a square button. "According to the diagrams it is a warp speed."

The professor turned around and addressed everyone. "This may be a rocky start. Make sure that you are secure. Everyone ready? Here we go!"

The ship slowly lifted off the ground and continued to rise upward. "Michael, keep an eye out on the camera system for your pilot buddies."

"Okay professor, will do." The ship rose to about two thousand feet when O'Dell noticed two F16's approaching. "Hit it professor!" O'Dell screamed.

"Hold on everyone," Simonson said as he hit the warp speed button then shut it off immediately.

"Why did you stop," Sara asked.

"We have to navigate at a slower pace through the asteroid belt," Simonson replied.

"So hit it until we get there," Sara suggested.

"We're there my dear," Simonson said as he pointed to the large camera screen. Everyone gathered around to see millions of rocks everywhere. Some were as small as a baseball others were miles wide. "You see my dear, the warp speed is extremely fast. Does anyone feel lighter?" Simonson asked.

Everyone agreed that they didn't feel lighter. "No, why?" Sara asked. "Amazing," Simonson said. "This ship has gravitational settings. We should actually be weightless right now, but the ship is set for Earth's gravity."

2

"What are we going to do about those asteroids? Won't they tear us to shreds?" Michelle asked.

"I don't think so," Simonson replied. "We can dodge the big ones and the small ones should bounce right off this strong metal."

As they entered the meteor belt, the ship was pounded with small rocks. The noise was tremendous. It was worse than any hailstorm. The professor began to teach O'Dell and Wesley the simplistic navigational system. "We should break into two groups," Simonson said. "We need half to fly the ship and the other half should rest until it's their turn to fly the ship. I'll take Coy, Paul, Stephen, Michelle, and Tabitha. Wesley and Michael can fly the second shift with Sara, William, and Jade. You should probably go into the large chamber and rest. We will wake you in twelve hours to switch. Everyone agreed to Simonson's plan. O'Dell, Jade, and Wesley fell instantly to sleep. Sara and William chatted awhile. They were having trouble sleeping with the rock storm rattling the ship.

Simonson continued to steer the ship away from the large meteors for the next twelve hours. After the twelve hours was up, he sent Tabitha to go wake the others. She entered the large chamber and woke them all up.

"Feels like I just went to sleep," Sara said. "I see the racket hasn't stopped."

"No," Tabitha agreed. "I think it has actually gotten worse." They switched crews and continued on their journey. This continued day after day. The meteors were relentless. The pounding had become a regular sound.

3

O'Dell was flying when he noticed a large asteroid ahead. It was the size of a large planet. He sent Sara to wake the others. She came back with Professor Simonson as the others slowly joined them. "Look," O'Dell said. "It will take forever to go around this thing."

"There is a hole in it down there," Wesley said as he pointed at the screen. The hole in the meteor was about two miles wide and a half-mile high.

"We can't be sure that the hole goes all the way through," Simonson said.

"If it doesn't we will have room to turn around," Wesley pointed out.

Simonson put his hand on his chin as he sighed. "Sara, you're funding this mission. It's your choice."

"No Professor," she answered. "We are all in this together. We should vote."

"Okay," O'Dell said. "Everyone that wants to go around it raise your hand." Michelle, Tabitha, Paul, Tom, and Simonson all raised their hands. "Now how about going through the hole?" Michael asked as he raised his hand. Jade, William, Wesley, Coy, Steve, and Sara joined him. "I guess we're going through it."

Michael positioned the ship at the entrance of the hole. As the ship entered, the sound of the pummeling rocks dissipated.

"Oh thank god," Sara said. "That has been killing me for days." Later on that day they exited the meteor. The pounding rocks started up again. They continued on for several days.

4

Simonson's crew was awoken and everyone gathered in the control room. "Where are we going?" Jade asked.

"We are going to the Alpha Centauri System," Simonson answered.

"Why?" Tabitha asked.

"Well." He said, "We want to find a planet that is capable of supporting life. The Alpha Centauri System contains three stars: Alpha Centauri A, Alpha Centauri B, and Proxima. In order for a planet to support life, its sun must pass five tests." The professor then gave them the lecture of a lifetime. In high school all the students would have fallen asleep, but the crew was now living in space so this interested them.

"The first test is to ensure the stars maturity and stability. The star must fuse hydrogen into helium at the core, generating light and heat. All three stars in the Alpha Centauri System pass this test." The professor pushed his glasses up on his round nose. He clearly loved the idea of teaching everyone.

"The second test is that the star must have the right spectral type. This determines how much energy a star emits. Hotter stars burn out too fast. Cooler ones don't have enough energy to support liquid water. A spectral type of G is perfect. Late F and early K are possible but less likely to support life. Alpha Centauri A has a spectral type of G2 and is perfect for supporting life. Alpha Centauri B is a K1 so it is possible but not as likely. Proxima has a spectral type of M that is far too cold. This is too bad for us because of the three it is the closest."

"We can still reach the other two right?" Coy asked.

"Oh yes," Simonson answered. Then he continued with the lecture. "The third criteria is that the star's brightness can't vary so much that it fries or freezes its inhabitants. Both Alpha Centauri A and B pass this test. Proxima has bursts that triple its output; therefore it fails this test also. The forth test is that the star must be old enough to give life a chance to develop. Our sun is 4.6 billion years old. Alpha Centauri A and B are each about five to six billion years old. They pass this test. Proxima once again fails. It is less than a billion years old. The last test is to have enough metals present in the star to allow the formation of a planet. Alpha Centauri A and B both pass this test. I have no clue whether Proxima passes or fails this test, but it doesn't matter anyway. We are headed to a planet that revolves around Alpha Centauri A. The planet seems to be the right distance from it to support life."

5

Suddenly, the pounding from the meteors had stopped. The camera screen revealed empty space ahead of them. "We're out of the asteroid belt," Wesley said.

Simonson switched places and began his shift. "Hold on everyone, I'm going to warp speed," he said as he pushed the button. They continued on their journey for the next two months. Very little was said to each other about the details of their personal lives. Over two months together and hardly anyone had opened up. Maybe they were preoccupied with the amazing mission they were on. Perhaps there was a trust issue. In fact, there was hardly any talking except for Simonson's occasional lectures and Wesley just being Wesley.

Simonson was in control when he noticed they were approaching the planet. "Can you go wake the others?" he asked Coy who gladly obliged. The others joined him in the navigation center.

"We did it," Sara cheered.

"We didn't do anything yet," Michael said. "We still have to land." The planet was seemingly all blue.

"There is water," William pointed out.

"Yes," Simonson said. "Unfortunately, that is all that I see. We need to land and we certainly can't do it on water."

"Over there," Paul said as he pointed on the screen. They were still a good distance from the planet. The chunk of land looked small from where they were. It was actually about the size of Texas. Simonson set his sights for the large island and began to close in.

Chapter Six:
The Planet

1

As they descended, Professor Simonson was overjoyed to see a forest. *'We've done it,'* he thought. *'We've found life beyond Earth.'* The ship dropped lower and lower as they looked for an opening to land. The controls suddenly locked up. "Oh no!" Simonson yelled. "I can't control it!"

"Brace yourselves everyone," O'Dell yelled. They were descending just over the forest.

"Look," Wesley said as he pointed to the screen. "There is a field. Maybe we can clear the forest." The field was square in shape with one tree exactly in the middle of the field. They continued to descend. Branches from the trees began to scrape the bottom of the ship. There was a loud thump as the ship spiraled to the center of the field and crashed down next to the lone tree.

The crew was thrown all over the ship. O'Dell got up first. "Is everyone alright?" he asked.

Jade climbed to her feet. "I'm fine," she said. Steve and Coy got up and helped Michelle to her feet. Sara lifted her head with a moan. Wesley, William, and Tabitha helped Finch and Simonson.

"We did it!" Simonson said with excitement. "Everyone ready to go explore the new planet?"

"Shouldn't we check on the repairs of the ship?" Coy asked.

"We can do that later," Simonson answered. "Michael, bring your knife and gun for protection. We have no idea what we'll find out here."

"I have a knife too," Jade added. She had it strapped to her leg.

2

The professor opened the door and they all stepped out into the field. They walked toward the forest ahead of them. As they entered the field Tabitha stopped them. She was glaring at a fern on the ground. She was speechless for a second.

"What is it?" Paul asked.

"This plant hasn't been around for over seventy million years."

"Correction my dear," Simonson said. "It hasn't been around on Earth for over seventy million years."

Just then there was a loud rumble as the ground shook. "I think we should get back to the ship now," Michelle suggested.

"Let's go!" Michael yelled as they all ran toward the ship. The rumbling continued as they entered the ship and closed the door. They all gathered around and peered at the camera screen.

"That's amazing," Tabitha said, still in disbelief. "A plant that has been extinct for millions of years is existing here in the wild."

Everyone watched the screen eagerly as a deer entered the field. It was running but tripped at the entrance of the field. It was noticeably injured, enough to hamper its speed. It got back up and began to run. Suddenly a Tyrannosaurus Rex emerged from the forest chasing the deer. The deer made one final desperation leap. It was scooped up in mid-air by the large jaws of the dinosaur.

"No, that was amazing," Michelle said.

"Holy shit," Steve said softly as he stared at the massive beast eating its meal. He was entranced by the horrific scene. "What have we gotten ourselves into?"

"This is extraordinary!" the professor shouted with glee.

"Yeah, I'm glad you're happy," Steve said sarcastically. "What happens when we're on its menu?" A mixture of excitement and fear came over the crew, mostly fear. Only Professor Simonson was noticeably excited but everyone else was noticeably worried. The T-Rex finished its meal and shook the ground as it walked back into the forest. After awhile the rumbling disappeared.

3

"We have to fix the ship," Coy insisted.

"We just arrived on this marvelous planet and you want to leave already?" the professor protested.

"No. I want to be able to leave if we need to."

"Oh very well," Simonson replied.

Simonson, Coy, Michael, and Wesley crept outside and assessed the damage. "Hey," Wesley said from the back of the ship. "I have some bad news. We punctured the fuel tank."

Michael, Coy, and Tom joined him on the back side of the ship.

"That doesn't look that bad," Coy said. "I can fix that."

"That's great," Wes said sarcastically. "Can you also magically put the fuel back in. I don't exactly see a fuel station around here. Maybe it's left of the T-Rex!"

"Calm down," Simonson said. "Maybe there is intelligent life here that could help us."

Wesley shook his head. *'He definitely isn't talking about Coy.'* Wesley looked over at the large man who was examining the fuel cell. "Sorry professor, I don't remember any intelligent life forms during the age of dinosaurs," Wesley stated.

"True, but there weren't deer either," Simonson answered. "Mammals didn't arrive until later. You must remember this isn't Earth. Things are very different here. Look up at the sky," Tom said. Wesley looked up to see Alpha Centauri A. It was this planet's sun. It looked just like our sun. To its right however, was Alpha Centauri B. It appeared about one eighth the size of Alpha Centauri A. It was awkward to see two suns. The suns were going down over the horizon. Night was coming.

"We should go inside and explore in the morning," O'Dell suggested. Simonson was so eager to explore this planet, but he knew that Michael was right. They joined the others inside and divulged the plan to explore in the morning.

"Are you kidding me?" Steve disagreed. "Did you not see that giant creature scoop up the deer?"

"That is exactly why we want to explore," Simonson said. "We need to learn our surroundings. It will help us protect ourselves."

"Do you really think anything will help protect ourselves from a T-Rex?"

"Well I want to go tomorrow," William said. "I could get some great pictures."

"We should all go for protection," Sara said. Everyone agreed, even Steve who was hesitant at first. Darkness fell as everyone settled in the ship. There were only ten beds and someone would have to share for the first time. Sharing a twin mattress would be quite tight.

"Do we have any volunteers to share a bed?" Simonson asked.

"I volunteer to sleep on the floor," Wesley said. "It helps my back anyway."

"That works," Sara said.

"Look," O'Dell said as he pointed to the camera screen. "No moon. It's going to be extremely dark out there at night with no moon."

"We should search for a stream tomorrow," Simonson suggested. "We should also consider hunting. If we're going to be here for a little while, we will need food and water. Our supplies won't last forever."

"What are you, on vacation?" Steve asked angrily. "You said that there might be intelligent life to help us."

"Yes, but we have to be prepared for the worst."

"Let's wake early and search for a stream," Sara said. Everyone went to sleep on what became a restless night for all. Some were excited about the possibilities. Others were hearing sounds outside.

Chapter Seven:
Exploration

1

The next day everyone woke up early. O'Dell opened the ship's door to a warm sunny morning. Everyone was startled by a chirping sound.

"What's that?" Sara whispered.

"I don't know," Michael answered. Everyone went to the camera screen and saw a dinosaur eating leaves from the tree. It was about seven feet tall. It stood on two strong legs and had a long neck.

"It's a Struthiomimus!" Michelle said.

"Is that good or bad?" Sara asked.

"Well," she answered, "I'm not sure. We have always believed it was a meat eater but a harmless one. It is a scavenger that only eats insects and carrion."

"I think our theory is wrong," William said. "It appears to be eating grass and leaves. It looks like a plant eater to me."

"How could we have been wrong all these years? I want to get a closer look," Michelle said as she began to walk out the door toward the dinosaur. The Struthiomimus looked at her, chirped, and ran off with a blaze of speed.

"Good thing it's a plant eater," Sara said. "That thing is fast."

"We should all get ready for a marvelous day of exploration," Simonson said with joy. "It is time to see how else our scientists have been wrong."

"Yes," O'Dell said. "We must prepare ourselves. It's not a game out here." O'Dell tossed William his knife. "I have a gun, figured I'd spread the wealth."

"Gee thanks," William said. "I feel real safe against a T-Rex with this."

"It's better than just your pen," O'Dell said.

"Yeah, yeah. Let's go."

"We need to do our exploring in a precise manor," Tom said. "We will call the direction Alpha Centauri rises east. In this instance, the tree is just to the north of our ship. Now, we are surrounded by forest. Do we want to go north, east, south, or west?"

"I'll pass on south," William said. Everyone looked at him strangely. "What? That's where the T-Rex came from yesterday."

"There was a song by the Pet Shop Boys that said 'Go west, life is peaceful there.' Maybe we should go west?" Sara said.

"Are you serious?" William asked. "Led Zeppelin also sang Stairway To Heaven. I don't want to end up there."

"William," Sara said with a smile. "Don't fear the reaper. Lets go west."

2

Everyone finally agreed and they began to walk toward the forest to the west. They reached the edge of the forest that was rather thick at the entrance. They had to walk single file. O'Dell led with his gun out in front. Tom, Paul, Michelle, Tabitha, Coy and Steve followed him in order. Wesley was next in line followed by Sara and William with his camera. Jade brought up the rear with her knife in hand. After several minutes of walking O'Dell stopped. He turned to the others and put his finger to his lips to silence them. Then he pointed ahead. There was a dinosaur that was knee high. It was walking on two legs in a giant nest of eggs. The eggs were about six inches long. William snapped a photo of the tiny dinosaur.

"Is that a baby?" Coy asked.

"No," Michelle said. "It's an adult Compsognathus."

Coy looked back at her confused. "How does a dinosaur that size pop out an egg that big?"

Michelle chuckled softly. "Those aren't its eggs silly!"

'Genius at work once again,' Wesley thought.

Then, they heard loud footsteps coming their way. The Compy grabbed an egg and ran off. The footsteps became faster, almost a jogging pace.

"Should we run?" Sara asked,

"Too late," Wesley said.

"Look," Michelle said. "There's momma. It's a Hadrosaurus."

"Translation?" Sara asked snottily.

"Plant eater," Michelle answered. "She shouldn't bother us as long as we stay away from that nest."

The Hadrosaurus was almost as tall as the T-Rex. William snapped another photo as the group careful walked around the nest at a distance.

"I could have made an awesome omelet out of one of those eggs," Steve said.

"We still have food left!" Sara griped. "I don't want to eat dinosaur until I have to."

"What has gotten into her?" Tabby whispered to Michelle who shrugged her shoulders. "She seems bitchy."

3

After another hour of walking they reached a swamp. The water was only knee deep but was very dark and murky. Nothing in the water was visible. As William stepped up onto a log Jade stopped him. "Don't move," she said. He looked up to see a Brontosaurus. He realized it wasn't a log he was standing on. It was this mammoth beast's tail.

Sara was frightened until she heard Michelle whisper over to her; "Plant eater."

William snapped a photo of the imposing beast. The Brontosaurus turned its head and long neck. It looked at William who was still on its tail. The massive beast flung its tail. William fell off as everyone else tried to jump out of the way. The tail hit Sara, Paul, Tom, and Coy and sent them flying into the mud. The Brontosaurus let out a loud roar and walked off. The water rippled with its thunderous steps. Sara climbed to her feet and wiped mud from her face. She was covered from head to toe.

Jade began laughing, which instantly annoyed Sara. "It's not funny bitch!" Sara yelled with rage.

"I found it rather amusing," Jade replied calmly. Coy and Paul helped Tom up. They were covered in mud also.

"Shit," William said. "The camera is broken. I think I can save the film though." He left the camera on the ground as he placed the film in his pocket.

"Well," Tom said. "I guess we have to be more careful."

4

They continued on. After another hour a light was visible through the trees. It was the end of the swamp. They exited the swamp and were on a beach. Beyond the beach was an endless ocean. Way out in the water was a giant fin sticking into the air. "That dorsal fin has to be fifteen feet high," Tom said. "Imagine how big that creature is."

"I don't care how big it is," Tabby said. "I know I'm not going swimming though."

"Well we can't go any further this way," O'Dell said.

"We should head back to the ship," Tom suggested. They all reentered the swamp. On the way back through the swamp they came across the Brontosaurus. William was amazed that he stood on this massive beasts tail and wasn't injured. He wasn't about to do it again though. They all kept a safe distance as they passed. The Brontosaurus looked their way and snorted. William could see the green mist viciously fly out of its nostrils. After that the giant beast ignored them.

5

When they were halfway back to the ship there were two Compies up ahead. The Compies noticed the group approaching. One of the small dinosaurs hopped up onto a fallen tree that lay across their path. Suddenly it lunged at Michelle. Michael fired his rifle and hit it in the chest. It dropped immediately. Michelle had blood speckles on her face. The second Compy ran toward them. Jade threw her knife and it stuck dead center in the Compy's chest. It dropped to the ground as blood slowly ran from the wound. Sara was laughing as she pointed to Michelle's face. Michelle simply wiped her face off with her sleeve.

"Oh it's funny now that it's not you?" Jade asked angrily.

"Yeah," Sara said snidely. "It's always funny when it's not me. I'd be laughing if it were you."

"You'd get knocked the fuck out too."

"Hey," William said. "Let's try to get along, at least until we get back to the safety of the ship."

Steve went over to the dead Compy that still had Jade's knife embedded in its chest. He grabbed Jade's knife and lifted the Compy with it.

"What are you doing?" Sara asked.

"This is my supper tonight," he replied.

"Gross!" she yelled.

"Hey, we have to get used to the taste sometime," Steve said. "We might be stuck here forever."

"Don't say that!" Sara shouted.

"Why princess? Your money will do us no good out here. You can't buy your way out of this one."

"Fuck you!" Sara yelled.

"Enough!" Jade shouted. "We can't be distracted by arguing. If you're not paying attention out here you become lunch."

"Jade's right," Michelle agreed. Sara just turned her head and continued walking.

They all made it safely to the ship and began to prepare their supper. Sara, Paul, and Wesley had fish sticks while the others ate Compy. "Not bad," Coy said.

"Yeah," Michelle joked. "Kind of tastes like chicken."

"That is some sick shit," Wesley said as he cringed.

"Try some Wes," Michelle said. "It's not bad."

"No thanks."

After dinner they all watched the setting suns, then went to sleep.

6

The next morning came and the explorers had breakfast and decided to try north today. They had walked for an uneventful two hours with no sight of a stream.

"So how do you know so much about dinosaurs?" Sara asked Michelle.

"I took a couple courses in college. I wanted to study all animals, not just the living."

"Guess what sweetheart, they live," Wesley joked.

Suddenly there was a stench in the air. "Something is burning," Simonson said. "Maybe there is a civilization ahead." They came upon a fire pit that was still smoldering.

There were four stakes in the ground around the fire pit. Each stake had a human skull on it. Michelle thought back to Biology class in high school where there was always a bright white skeleton at the front of the room. Skeletal Sally they called her. This was similar but alarmingly different. These were just skulls and they weren't bright white. They were a dull gray with black chars on them. Skeletal Sally was a fake skeleton that was helpful, these were real skulls and that was horrifying.

"What the hell is this?" Sara asked worriedly.

"Looks like cannibals," Tom said. "I'm overjoyed to see that we're not the only humans here."

"We may be the only friendly humans here," Steve said despairingly.

"Right, we should probably continue on before they return," Simonson suggested.

7

After another two hours the forest opened up to vast plains. The plains must have continued on for miles. The scenery was loaded with wildlife. "Okay Michelle, what are they all?" Sara asked. Michelle was in wonder at the view in front of her.

"Well, you remember the Struthiomimus," she said as she pointed to a group of five. There were about seven other dinosaurs next to the Struthiomimus. They looked similar but had a beak. Michelle referred to these as Gallimimus.

"Gallimimus are herbivores also?" Michelle said in disbelief. "I can't believe they are herbivores."

"They may have evolved differently on this planet than our own," Simonson stated. There was a large tank-like beast past them. It was about thirty feet long. It had a shell similar to a turtle. There was a huge club at the end of its tail. This was an Ankylosaurus. There was a herd of about fifteen other creatures next to it. They were about the same size and had three horns on their head, two above their eyes and one on their nose. The two above their eyes were about five feet long. Sara knew that these were Triceratops. There were also some white-tailed deer, zebras, and giraffes. They stood there for a while and took in the spectacular scene of wildlife. To Michelle it looked like an odd version of the Masai Mara.

8

They decided to turn around and head for home. As they approached the location of the cannibal camp O'Dell and Wesley scouted ahead. They quietly snuck through the bushes at a safe distance and peaked through. There were about thirty-five men around the campfire. They were dark skinned. Their faces were painted all white except two black lines extending vertically from the top and bottom of their lips. The lines were about half an inch thick. The top line extended up to the nose. The bottom line dropped to the chin. They were shirtless and wore deer hide skirts. There was a large stick suspended over the fire in a sis kebob fashion. It was a man that was attached to the stick. The man's flesh was beginning to form bubbles from the heat. "Dude, I'm gonna loose it," Wesley whispered as he clutched his stomach.

"Let's go back to the others," O'Dell said. O'Dell and Wesley returned to the group. "We need to go around," O'Dell said.

"Yeah, they are definitely unfriendly," Wes added. The explorers quietly circled around the camp at a safe distance. They continued on for another hour.

"What's that?" Jade asked.

"What?" William said.

"I heard something."

Suddenly there was a screeching sound. It was similar to a hawks cry. Two dinosaurs leaped out on each side of them. They were about seven feet tall on two legs. Each foot had a dewclaw that was about six inches long.

"Raptors!" Michelle yelled. Michael shot one in the throat. It dropped instantly. The other leaped at them. It landed on Steve, driving its dewclaw through his throat.

"Run!" O'Dell yelled. "It's too late for Steve." They began to run. The Raptor was content with feeding on Steve. They made it to the field and continued sprinting until they entered the ship.

Michelle was crying. William went over and put his arms around her. She wiped her tears. "Those weren't normal Raptors," she said.

"What do you mean?" William asked.

"They were huge compared to the size of a Velociraptor."

"They looked about as big as the ones in the movie Jurassic Park," William said.

"That was for cinematic effect. A real Raptor was only about three to four feet tall," Michelle said. "These Raptors must have evolved differently."

Simonson overheard their conversation and joined them. "This is very fascinating," he said. "We may have different species all together on this planet. The entire planet has evolved differently." "

Later that night they held a memorial service for Steve Hanson. Everyone said something nice about him. Afterward there was discussion about the continued search for a nearby stream. "I know that no one is in the mood to go exploring tomorrow, but it is something that we have to do," O'Dell stated.

"No way!" Sara screamed. "I'm not leaving the ship. I don't want one of those Raptors to kill me."

"If we don't find a creek, we're all going to die. We have supplies, but they were intended for the trip home. We can't keep cutting into those. We stand a much better chance against those Raptors if we're all together."

"Your right Michael," Sara agreed. "We'll continue in the morning."

9

The next morning came and the decision was to travel north. After an hours walk in the woods there was a rustling sound from up ahead.

"Coy, let's go see what it is," Michael suggested.

Coy nodded as they scouted ahead. They returned a few minutes later.

"It's one of those three-horns," Coy said.

"Triceratops?" Michelle asked.

"Yes," O'Dell confirmed.

"It shouldn't bother us as long as we keep our distance," Michelle said. They carefully walked around the Triceratops. It glanced their way then went back to eating ferns.

They continued on for another ten minutes before Jade stopped them. "Stop," she said. "Do you hear that?"

"No," William said. Then they all heard it. The ferns and bushes were moving all around them. Suddenly they were surrounded by creatures. There were seven of them. They looked like men but had hair all over their bodies. Their faces looked like that of an ape. Jade threw her knife and hit one of the apemen in the throat. It fell instantly. William threw Michael's knife and hit one in the leg. Michael shot one in the head and ceased its existence. This was the breaking point for thc apemen. The gun is what made them turn and run away. The apeman William hit pulled the knife out of its leg and dropped it. Then it hobbled off.

"What the hell were they Michelle?" Sara asked.

"I don't know but I don't want to meet them again."

"They must be a species exclusively located on this planet," Simonson said. "This is marvelous. I'm sure this planet has many mysteries to unlock."

"Yeah that's great doc," Wesley said. "I just hope were all around to see them. We already lost Steve."

10

They continued on for another hour. "What's that?" Jade asked.

"I wish you'd stop that," Wesley said. "Every time you hear something we narrowly escape death."

"Get it right," Jade said. "You narrowly escape death because I hear something. Don't blame me, thank me. This is different anyway. It sounds like water." They continued on to find a stream directly ahead. It was about twenty-five feet wide and two feet deep. The water was clear and the stream moved at a nice pace.

"Now we know where to find water," Tom said. He dipped his hand down into the stream and scooped some water up. He raised it to his mouth and drank. "It's not bad."

"Should we keep traveling north?" O'Dell asked.

"Yes," Tom said. I want to know our surroundings. Plus, finding water doesn't solve our fuel problem." They crossed the river and continued on for another hour before reaching a grassy meadow. It was about fifty feet wide. Past the meadow clouds and water were all that was visible. The ground seemed to disappear. They approached the edge with caution. They looked down to see they were on the edge of a rocky cliff. The ocean was down about two hundred feet. It was vast and beautiful. There were large birds flying out over the ocean. As one of the flying giants drew closer they realized it wasn't a bird.

"It's a Pteranodon," Michelle pointed. It had a crowned head. The wingspan was about twenty-five feet. It swooped down and pulled a fish off the top of the water. The Pteranodon was flying at a height of about eighty feet when a giant shark emerged straight up from the water. It plucked the Pteranodon out of the sky. At its peak the shark's tail was still in the water.

"That thing must be over a hundred feet long," Finch said.

"Like I said before," Tabitha laughed. "I'm not going swimming."

"Well we can't go farther north," O'Dell said. "Let's head back to camp."

11

They were about halfway back when they heard loud screeching noises.

"Get down!" O'Dell yelled. They all hid behind a fallen tree and waited. The ground rumbled with footsteps. Two Struthiomimus ran by at a blazing speed. The bird-like dinosaurs were being chased by a T-Rex. It came within twenty feet of the fallen tree but continued chasing the Struthiomimus. The explorers waited until the T-Rex was a safe distance from them before they continued home.

They returned to the ship and had supper. Afterward Coy went over and sat next to Sara. "Why did you decide to come here?" he asked. "I mean; you have all the money you need. You can buy anything you want."

"Money doesn't mean a thing Coy. I would give it all up if I could have my mom and dad back. I had nothing left on Earth. I wanted to do something that would've made my dad proud."

"Well you did it," Coy said. "We're here. He definitely would be proud of you."

"No," Sara said. "This trip wasn't worth it. I got Steve killed and the rest of us are stranded here waiting for the dinosaurs to pick us off one by one."

"You didn't get Steve killed. He had the choice of not coming along."

"He didn't have a choice Coy. I offered him a million dollars. Who would turn that down?"

"Jade did," Coy answered.

"Yeah, well Jade's not normal," Sara said as Jade walked by.

"I heard that," Jade said with a smile. "Don't make me come over there and kick your snotty little ass," she said as she laughed.

"Besides," Coy said. "We all knew the dangers involved with this trip."

"Really," Sara said. "You knew there were dinosaurs here?"

"Well, no. But we knew it was dangerous. Don't blame yourself. None of us do."

"Thanks Coy," she said as she hugged him.

"Tomorrow we should head east," Simonson said as he gathered everyone's attention.

"Why," Tabitha said. "We already found a stream."

"Yes, but there might be a closer one. Also we should know our surroundings. We know everything to our west and south until we reach ocean. To the North we have traveled as far as the Great Plains. It is only fitting that we see what surrounds us to the east."

Everyone agreed and they decided they would leave early in the morning.

Chapter Eight:
The Dambroo

1

The next morning everyone was startled when the ship began to rock.

"What the hell is going on?" Sara yelled. O'Dell looked out the door and began to chuckle. "What is so funny?" Sara asked.

"It appears that our Ankylosaurus friend has an itch and he's using our ship to scratch it."

"Aw man," Coy said as he walked outside. "Hey, leave our ship alone," Coy yelled. The Ankylosaurus calmly looked over at Coy and swung its powerful clubbed tail. Coy dove out of the way. The tail hit the ship and sent it sliding for five feet. Coy ran back inside out of breath. "I think I'm gonna leave him alone."

"Good idea," Sara said as they all laughed. They waited inside for the Ankylosaurus to leave. After it left, they exited the ship and walked toward the forest in the east. As soon as they entered they saw a large dinosaur. It was about twenty-five feet long and had large plates up its back. It walked on four legs and had four spikes on its tail. Each spike was about three feet long. "Stegosaurus," Michelle said. "Plant eater," she elaborated. It ignored them as they walked past it at a distance.

2

After a two hour walk in the forest they reached a great stonewall. It was about twenty-five feet high and five hundred feet long. "What is this?" William asked.

"Whatever it is, it has to have been made by intelligent life," Simonson said. They followed the wall until they came to a set of doors. The doors were about ten feet tall and made from wood. Painted on the outside of each door were two spears crossed. They formed an X with the points facing up.

"This is a civilization!" Simonson cheered.

"Don't be so happy professor," William said. "Not all civilizations are friendly to strangers.

"Might as well find out," Wesley said as he pounded on the doors.

"What the hell are you doing?" Sara screamed. "Are you insane!" The two doors slowly opened. There was a small village inside. Just inside the doors were two guards. Each of them had a spear.

"We come in peace," Simonson said. The two guards looked at each other confused. Then the guard on the right yelled out, "Watoo!" Four more guards ran toward them.

"Oh shit," Wesley said. The guards took Michael's gun away. They also grabbed the knives off of William and Jade. The guards stood behind the crew with their spears pointed at the explorer's backs. Wesley could feel the fine point delicately touching his lower back. The guards led the explorers through town in this manner. There were stone houses on both sides of the street. The street was actually more like a large walkway. There were obviously no motorized vehicles. This civilization was relatively primitive. Some villagers were outside of their houses as the explorers were led through town. They stared as they walked past.

"What do we do?" Sara asked.

"Relax for now," Simonson said. "I think if they wanted to kill us they would have already done it." Simonson was glancing all around. These people, though primitive were far more advanced than the apemen and cannibals. They had white skin and wore clothes. Most had shorts and shirts. The explorers were led to the center of town to a beautiful woman. She was sitting on a throne on top of a series of steps. The throne was guarded on all four sides.

"It is their queen," Simonson said. They were led up the steps and placed directly in front of her. She was a brunette. She wore some sort of chest guard out of metal. On bottom she wore a short fur skirt.

"Fatu wat?" the queen asked. The explorers looked at each other confused.

Simonson stepped forward, but was stopped by the crossed spears of the guards.

"Matai," the queen said as she motioned for them to lower their spears. They lowered them as Simonson put his hand on his chest. "Tom," he said.

"Tom?" she repeated.

He nodded. "Tom," he said.

She seemed confused by the nodding. She put her hand on her chest and said, "Laza."

"Laza," Tom repeated.

"Laza," she said as she nodded with a smile on her face.

'Well, these people are intelligent,' Tom thought. *'She learned immediately that nodding means yes.'*

Michelle stepped up and touched her chest. "Michelle," she said.

"Meeshell," Queen Laza replied.

Michael did the same.

"Mikell," she replied. The explorers introduced themselves one by one.

Tom then pointed to the whole group and stated, "American."

"Mareecon," Queen Laza replied.

"No," Tom said as he shook his head. "American."

"Uh-mare-ee-can," the queen repeated.

"Yes," Tom said as he nodded.

Queen Laza pointed all around her to her people. "Dambroo," she said.

"Dom-brew," Tom repeated.

"Yes," she said as she nodded and laughed. She was rather young for a queen, possibly in her thirties. Tom reached out his hand in front of her. She copied his motion and brought her hand forward to meet his. They shook hands.

3

The explorers were then allowed to walk around the town escorted by two guards. The spears were down now as the environment was far more peaceful.

One of the Dambroo citizens came over to William. It was a young man. The man lightly tugged on William's shirt. William took his shirt off and held it in his hand. With his other hand he pointed to the gentlemen's spear. The man handed William his spear. William in turn handed the man his shirt. They traded.

"Dako," the man said.

"Dako," William repeated. He assumed that it meant 'thank you'. He was correct.

"I think we should return here at a later date," Tom said.

"Yes," O'Dell agreed. "We should continue east."

They walked to the village doors where they were handed their weapons back. William tossed the knife to Coy. He no longer needed it because he now owned a spear. They entered the forest and continued east. After two hours the trees gave way to sand. This wasn't a beach though; it was a desert. It stretched as far as the eyes could see. They continued east through the desert for an hour before deciding to turn around. There was still no end in sight. On their way back Coy spotted something. "What's that," he asked as he pointed into the distance. It was a living creature about the size of a car and it was headed their way. Michael raised his gun. As it got closer everyone saw that it was a huge scorpion.

"Michelle did this thing live when the dinosaurs did?" Wesley asked.

"I've never heard of anything like this. It must have evolved differently on this planet."

They all became quite worried as the creature drew near. Michael shot and missed. The scorpion's tail, equipped with stinger came down toward Jade. She dove out of the way. The tail hit the sand spraying grains into the air and leaving an eight-inch hole. O'Dell shot again. This time he hit the scorpion's tail. It quickly scampered off. Jade got up and brushed the sand off her legs and chest.

"That was amazing," Simonson said.

"I know," William agreed. "She's fast. I thought for sure she was getting impaled."

"No, no. I'm talking about the scorpion. There are creatures on this planet that we've never imagined. I can't wait to explore this place fully."

"You can't be serious," Wesley said.

"Well how else will we find fuel for the ship?" Simonson said with a smile.

They continued walking home.

"Thanks for the vote of confidence," Jade said sarcastically.

"What? It did almost impale you," William said.

"Li Wu strikes faster than that slow ass scorpion."

"Looked pretty fast to me," William said. Jade just shook her head. They made it safely to the ship only seeing a passive Ankylosaurus along the way. It ignored them as they walked by at a distance.

4

When they reached the ship Tom called a group meeting. "I think we need to start hunting every day. We will need to conserve our canned goods for the trip home."

"I agree," Michael said.

"We'll never make it home!" Sara snapped.

"Thanks for the optimism," Jade said.

"Well, we have no fuel!" Sara yelled. "The Dambroo may have spears and knives but I sure as hell didn't see a Mobil station. Did you?"

"If you want to lose hope go right ahead, but don't bring the rest of us down!"

"Enough!" Michael interrupted. "We need to stick together out here. We can't be arguing over this. It's not doing us any good. The only thing we can count on out here is each other."

"You're right," Jade said. "But I'm making it home."

"We should gather what we don't need and trade with the Dambroo for whatever we can get that's useful," Paul suggested.

"Good idea," Michael said as he looked at his watch. "Does anyone else have a watch?" he asked.

"Why?" William asked.

"Well, the first day we were here it got dark at ten o'clock. It's five o'clock now and it's already getting dark out there."

"Oh yes," Simonson said. "I forgot to tell you. The planet spins at about the same rate that Earth does, but it is a little smaller. It only takes approximately twenty-three hours for it to revolve. Don't you feel lighter?"

"No," O'Dell said.

"Well it is only about a eight pound difference per two hundred pounds."

"Is there anything else you didn't tell us Professor," Wesley asked. "Are we all breathing in toxic gasses or catching some rare disease or anything else we don't know about?"

"I'm not sure," he answered. "But if the creatures that are hear can handle it we should be able to."

"Good," Wesley said.

"Unless they evolved differently," Tom joked.

"Don't play me Doc," Wesley said. "I can't take much more."

Later, everyone had gathered the things that could be parted with for trade.

"What's that sound?" Jade asked. The others began to hear it. It was a humming sound that was getting louder. Everyone went outside in the darkness and gathered by the ship. There was a distant green glow coming from the forest to the north. The humming became louder and what was once a large green glow became about fifty smaller green lights. As the lights exited the forest and entered the field toward them Michelle gasped.

"They are some form of giant lightning bug," she said. Each one was about a foot long. As the lightning bugs flew over there head they created a light breeze. This was a peaceful and spectacular display.

'This is simply enchanting,' Simonson thought. The display lasted about a minute then they were gone.

"That was beautiful," Sara said.

"This place is not only dangerous, but it also has many pleasant surprises," Simonson said. Everyone went inside and turned in for the night.

Chapter Nine:
Chores

1

The next morning O'Dell called a meeting. "We should split up today, but we should never be alone."

"Yes, we have plenty of things that need to be done today," Simonson added. "I'll take Paul and Tabitha with me to the Dambroo village to trade. We also need to hunt for food, gather water, and build a fire pit."

"I don't feel so good," Wesley said. "Is it okay if I stay at the ship today?"

"Certainly," Simonson said. "Rest up and get better."

"That's bullshit Wes," Sara said. "You just want to get out of doing work."

"Think what you want, I feel like shit."

"I'll hunt," O'Dell said to break the tension.

"Great," Simonson said. "Who's going with him?"

"I'll go with him," Michelle said as she walked over next to O'Dell.

"Who wants to go to the stream and gather water?" Tom asked.

"I'll get the water," Jade said.

"I'll go with her," William spoke up.

"Okay," Tom said. "That leaves Coy and Sara to make us a fire pit. Now does everyone have ample protection?"

"We're staying close to the ship," Coy said. "We should be fine with the knife that William gave me."

"I've got Jade and a spear," William laughed.

"Do you know how to use that spear?" Jade asked.

"Yeah, I think I can figure it out."

"Good," Jade said. "Keep yourself alive. I'm not here to baby-sit."

"Will we be alright Tom," Paul asked.

"The Dambroo village isn't that far. We will get weapons when we get there." Tabitha and Paul were carrying backpacks full of the crew's items.

Michael and Michelle went off to the west toward the swamp. Jade and William headed to the south toward the stream with two buckets. Tom, Paul, and Tabitha headed east toward the Dambroo village. Coy and Sara went to the north. Wesley went inside and slept.

2

"I remember there were some large rocks on the edge of the forest over here," Sara said. She was right. There were some nice rocks suitable for a fire pit. Coy began to grab the rocks as Sara watched.

"Aren't you going to help?" he asked.

"Yeah, I'll get the wood."

"You want me to get all these rocks by myself?"

"You're a big boy, you can handle it." Coy grabbed another rock and angrily headed back toward the ship. Sara began to gather sticks.

3

Meanwhile, in the forest to the west Michael was quietly sneaking around. Michelle stayed close to him and looked around in all directions. She wanted to make sure they were hunting, not being hunted. Michael slowly crouched down when he spotted a deer twenty yards away. He fired and the bullet hit the deer in the shoulder. It took three steps and dropped. He and Michelle were approaching it as he heard the bushes rustling. He fell to the ground behind a bush and pulled Michelle down with him. A Raptor leaped out from the weeds and began feeding on the deer. Michael grabbed Michelle's hand and quietly led her away. They stopped when they were a safe distance away from the Raptor.

"What about our deer?" Michelle asked. "That Raptor is eating our deer."

"I'd rather it be the deer than us. We'll find something else."

4

Tom, Paul, and Tabby arrived at the Dambroo village where they were welcomed. They began to trade their jewelry and other meaningless belongings. After a short time they were able to acquire a sword, two machetes, three spears, a fish net, and an ax. When they were done trading, two guards approached them. The guards led them to Queen Laza. A slim, well-toned brunette accompanied the queen. She was wearing a deer fur bikini and carried a spear. "Kiya," the queen said as she placed her hand on the girl's shoulders. Tom, Tabby, and Paul repeated her name then introduced themselves. Queen Laza pointed all around her to the village. "Wakai," she said. "Laza wakai, Kiya wakai, Dambroo wakai."

"I think wakai means home or village," Tabby said.

Then the queen put her hand on Kiya and said, "American wakai."

"I think she wants us to take Kiya to our home," Tabby said.

"I think that is a great idea," Simonson said as he nodded to the queen. "You are picking up on their language pretty quick, Tabby. Maybe you can learn the Dambroo language and teach Kiya English."

They began to leave with Kiya next to them. Tabby turned around to the queen. "Dako," Tabby said. Dako was the Dambroo word for 'thank you'.

"Sarto Kai," Queen Laza replied. This meant 'you're welcome.'

5

William and Jade had reached the stream. They each filled their bucket with water. "How come you've been so quiet?" William asked.

"What is there to talk about?"

"Well," he said. "What about just a friendly conversation?"

"In order to have a friendly conversation I feel that you should actually be friends," she answered.

"Gee thanks," William said.

Suddenly Jade was swept off her feet by a rope trap. The pail of water fell to the ground and spilled. She was dangling upside-down from a tree. Two apemen charged toward them from behind the bushes. William dropped the bucket and stabbed the first one with his spear as it attacked him. The other one was heading for Jade. William pulled the spear out of the dead ape-man and threw it toward the other one. The spear impaled the ape-man's throat ending its life. William walked under Jade who was right above his head. She unstrapped her knife and cut the rope. She fell into William's arms. He was holding her like a husband holds his new bride as she's carried through the door of their hotel room.

"Put me down," she said.

"Is that you're thanks?" he asked.

"Thanks? If you hadn't been talking to me, I would've seen the trap. Now put me down," she insisted.

"Okay," he said as he dropped her on the ground. Jade hit the ground hard and swung her leg around tripping William. He fell to the ground next to her. She climbed on top, straddled him and raised her knife.

"If you ever drop me again like that I'll kill you."

"Boy this is nice and intimate with you on top of me like this," he joked.

"Don't get used to it," she replied as she stood up. She lowered her hand and grabbed his and helped him up. "Let's go get more water," Jade said as she grabbed her empty pail.

"You need to lighten up Jade. I'm not your enemy, you know. You can trust me."

"I trust nobody," she said coldly.

"Why? Is it that hard to trust?"

"I've made it this far without trusting, no need to start now."

William shook his head and filled his pail with water.

6

Coy continued to retrieve rocks as Sara stayed by the edge of the forest gathering sticks. "You don't have to be rude to people you know." Coy said.

"I'm not rude. I'm just to the point," Sara answered.

"You might not want to piss off the people you need."

"The people I need? I don't need anyone," she said as she walked into the forest.

"Where are you going?" Coy asked.

"I'm getting sticks," she yelled. "Leave me the hell alone!" As soon as she turned two cannibals jumped out of the bushes and grabbed her. She screamed as Coy threw the knife and hit one in the throat. The cannibal grabbed his throat as he fell to the ground. The other one released his grip on Sara and ran off. She fell to the ground and began crying. Coy walked over to her and helped her up. He held her as she cried into his shoulder. "Why did you help me right after I said that I didn't need you?"

"You may not be able to admit that you need me, and that's okay. But I know that I need you as well as all the others too," Coy said.

"I'm sorry," Sara said. "I do need you. I shouldn't have treated you like shit. I can't believe how kind and understanding you are even when people treat you bad. Let's go back to the ship. I'll help you build the fire pit."

7

Michael and Michelle hid behind a tree as they saw two Compies ahead. He raised his gun and fired. He hit one of the Compies and killed it. The other one attacked him before he could do anything. The gun fell out of his hand as the Compsognathus bit into his leg. Michelle grabbed a large rock and hit the Compy. It fell off Michael and looked up at Michelle. That was the last thing it saw as the rock came down again.

"Thanks," O'Dell said.

"Hey, we were both sent hunting. I can't let you have all the fun." They each threw a Compy over their shoulder and began to return to the ship.

8

Tom, Paul, Tabby, and Kiya made their way back to the ship. Tabby introduced Kiya to Coy and Sara who had the fire pit completed. Tabitha and Kiya entered the ship and woke Wesley up. Tabitha introduced Wesley to Kiya.

"I'm definitely not against having another pretty girl around here," Wesley said. The girls began teaching each other as much as they could about each other's languages, while Wesley went outside and helped Coy and Paul with the fire.

Sara had pulled Professor Simonson aside. "What is Kiya doing here?" she asked.

"Well, she will be staying with us for a while. Tabby is learning the Dambroo language and teaching Kiya English."

"So we have another mouth to feed?" Sara said in disagreement.

"Maybe," Simonson said. "But it's a mouth that knows an awful lot about this planet. I'm positive that Kiya will help us far more than she'll hinder us."

Coy had the fire going pretty good when he noticed Michael and Michelle entering the field. He could see that they each were carrying something and that Michael was limping badly. Coy ran over to help them.

9

Meanwhile, Jade and William were still an hour from camp. "So why did you become a kick boxer?" he asked her.

"I'm not giving you an interview."

"God! I'm not trying to get an interview. I didn't even try the whole time we were on the ship traveling through space. I'm just trying to talk to you. So why did you become a kick boxer? There must be some reason?"

"I don't want to talk about it."

"Okay, what do you want to talk about?" he asked.

"Nothing," she replied.

"Why?"

"That's just the way I am," she said.

"You know I've been to a lot of ISKA matches in my life and you're the best fighter I've ever seen."

"What are you doing?" Jade asked. "Are you trying to get into my pants?"

"No. Can't anyone give a compliment without having ulterior motives?"

"I'm sorry," she said. "Thank you for the compliment."

"You're welcome. Now was that so hard?"

"To be honest, yes. I'm more comfortable hating people and beating the crap out of them then I am talking to them and being friendly."

"Jade, I just want to get to know you. I want to be your friend. That's all."

"Fine," Jade said. "You want to know the real Jade Evans, I'll tell you. Don't you dare print anything I say in the damn paper or I'll never talk to you again."

"Deal," he said. "I promise I want to know you as a friend not as a journalist."

"My parents and brother were killed in a car accident when I was eight. I lived with my martial arts teacher Shidoshi Idori who was a friend of my father's and the closest thing I had left to a relative."

"I'm sorry," he said.

"Then, shortly after I turned eighteen Shidoshi Idori died of a heart attack. I continued to live on my own. Everyone I was ever close to, I lost. I don't need to get close to anyone anymore. It's not worth the pain of losing them."

"Jade, I appreciate you telling me all this. I know it isn't easy for you."

"This is our secret you got it?" she said defensively.

"Don't worry. I won't tell anyone. I'm just happy that you let me in," he replied as they left the woods and entered the field. They could see a small fire going.

The whole crew was outside around the fire except for Tabitha.

"Where's Tabby?" William asked.

"Her and Kiya are in the forest looking for some plant that will heal Michael's leg," Sara answered.

William glanced down at Michael's leg. "That looks pretty bad," William said.

"It's not that bad," O'Dell said. "Besides, the plant is supposed to help with infection."

"Hey wait," William said. "Who's Kiya?"

"She's our new pet," Sara said with a smile.

"Kiya is our new friend from the Dambroo village," Simonson explained. "She will be staying with us for awhile."

Sara pulled William to the side. "So," she whispered. "Did you have fun with the ice queen?"

William thought about that comment for a moment. Sara considered Jade to be frigid and distant. Maybe the entire group did. He knew she was just misunderstood though. "She's not really that bad. I see we get to have Compsognathus again,"

"Yeah, I think I'll actually try some," Sara said.

10

Kiya and Tabitha returned with the plant. Kiya was introduced to Jade and William. Then she walked over to Michael and started to undo his pants.

"Whoa," he said as he held his hands up. Kiya held the plant up and pointed to it.

"I understand," Michael said "but let's go in the ship. I don't want everyone to see my drawers man."

"Damn, I like her," Wesley joked. "Can I have one. I think my leg's hurtin' Yeah as a matter of fact it's hurtin' like a bitch. The pain shoots all the way up."

"Grow up Wes," Sara said. "I don't see how you ever get laid."

"Come on inside. I'll show ya sweet cheeks."

"No thanks," Sara said as she laughed.

Michael and Kiya went into the ship. He slid his pants down. The pain set in a little as the pants rubbed against the cut when they slid past. Kiya came over and sat next to him. She broke open the plant. Inside was a white milky liquid. She put some on her hand and started to rub the wound. The pain was severe. When she moved her hand she looked up and smiled at Michael. He looked down at her.

"Dako," he said.

"Your welcome," she replied. Michael was shocked.

"You can speak English?" he asked.

"Small English," she said.

"You mean a little English," Michael said as he pulled his pants up.

"Yes, Tabby teach me," she said as they walked back outside.

O'Dell walked over to Tabitha. "You've done an amazing job at teaching her English," he said.

"She is still learning, but the credit all belongs to her. She is a genius. She is picking it up so fast. At the same time, I'm struggling to learn her language."

Kiya continued to live with them and teach Tabby, as Tabby taught her. They all continued getting water from the stream and hunting for their food. Occasionally they were treated to deer for supper. Usually they had to settle for Compy. Compsognathus was the easiest thing to hunt because unlike deer, they weren't timid. They actually attacked even after seeing another Compy shot. The explorers and Kiya lived like this for the next two weeks. Michael's wound had healed and they had virtually no danger for those two pleasant weeks. William and Jade's friendship grew as she learned to trust him.

Chapter Ten:
Once Bitten

1

Everyone was sitting around the campfire. It was midday. Sara appeared to be in a bitchier mood than usual.

"We've been stuck out here for three weeks!" she yelled. "We'll never make it home."

"We have to think positive," William said. "I'm going to the stream to get some water. Who wants to go with me?"

"I'll go," Jade said. "William and Jade entered the south forest. They each had a pail in one hand and a spear in the other.

Michael, Coy, and Michelle went hunting. The others stayed at the ship.

William and Jade had made it halfway when he asked her, "so why did you offer to come with me?"

Jade dropped the pail and spear and approached him. She wrapped her arms around him. Her right hand went up to the back of his head. She looked him in the eyes. "Because you are so irresistible," she answered.

"I am?" he asked. Her hands released from around him and made their way to his chest.

"Yeah," she said as she laughed and shoved him to the ground. She stood over him and continued to laugh.

"That's not funny," he said. He got up and began to walk away.

"I was just joking around," Jade said.

"Yeah, well I don't like being teased."

Suddenly a snake dropped out of a tree above. It was black with yellow rings around it. It landed on William's shoulder and bit him in the shoulder blade. "Ah," he screamed as he shook it off. He stabbed it with his spear.

"Are you okay?" Jade asked.

"I think so," he replied as he took his shirt off.

"I think that we should go back to the ship," Jade said.

"Nonsense, I'm fine. Plus we're more than halfway to the stream."

"We don't know what kind of snake that was. I think we should be cautious and go back to the ship."

"No," he said stubbornly. "Let's go on."

"I'll tell you what; if you go back to the ship with me I'll give you a kiss," she said bribing him.

"I don't have time for you to tease me. Let's go get the stupid water."

"Please," Jade pleaded.

"Ok," he agreed. "But I want my kiss first."

"Fine," she said. She went over to him and put her hand on the back of his head. She pulled him into her and gave him a slow sensuous kiss. Their lips separated briefly but she pulled him back in. Then they separated. "Now," she said calmly. "Let's go."

Jade used his shirt to tie the spears together at the top with the pails. She carried them over her shoulder. They began walking but William felt dizzy. He had to put his arm around Jade's shoulder as she helped him walk.

2

Meanwhile Michelle, Coy, and O'Dell were still hunting. They were crouched behind a huge rock watching a deer draw near. It was about twenty feet away when Michael aimed his gun. Then, Michelle stood up and threw her spear. It soared through the air and impaled the deer in the neck. The deer ran about fifteen feet and dropped.

"What the hell did you do that for?" Michael yelled. "I had it in my sights. It could have run off if you missed."

"I didn't miss," Michelle said. "I just wanted to show you that I can hunt too."

"I guess you can!" Coy said. "Did you see that Mike? She didn't even need a gun."

"Shut up," he said angered that a girl outdone him. They approached the dead deer and Coy grabbed a leg.

"Where did you learn to throw a spear like that?" Coy asked.

"I learned on the Masai Mara," she replied.

"Oh please, shut up," Michael said. "Somebody shoot me."

"Well you have the gun," Coy said. "But I'm sure Michelle could spear you."

Michael grabbed the front legs with disgust. He did not like being showed up. Coy had the back legs as they half carried, half dragged supper back to the ship.

3

William had gotten worse. Jade was practically carrying him now. Finally they reached the field. Sara saw Jade dragging William and yelled to the others. "William's hurt," she yelled. Michael and Coy went out and each grabbed an arm. They carried him to the ship as Jade followed. They placed him on his bed as everyone gathered near.

"What happened?" Tom asked.

"He got bit by a snake," Jade said.

"What color did it look?" Kiya asked.

"It was black with yellow rings," Jade answered.

"Oh no," Kiya said. "It was a Tabero. They are deadly. Only the Sacharoo plant can save him."

"Where do we find this plant?" Jade asked.

"Only place I know is an island," Kiya answered.

"How far is this island?" Tom asked.

"From here to the Dambroo and twice as long as that," she answered.

"That is like six hours," O'Dell said.

"We must get going," Kiya said. "He'll be dead by sunset."

"But that's like twelve hours away," Sara said.

"No room for error," O'Dell said. "Let's go!"

"Someone must stay with him," O'Dell said. "Who will stay?"

"I'll stay," Jade said.

Michelle, Paul, and Tom also decided to stay behind.

4

O'Dell, Kiya, Tabby, Wesley, Sara, and Coy set off for the Dambroo village. It would take them two hours east to get to the Dambroo village. If Kiya were right it would be another four hours north to the lake. Maybe if the explorers came home southwest they could make it in time to save William. There was about eleven and a half hours of daylight left.

William looked up at Jade who was standing over him. The two of them were alone. Tom, Michelle, and Paul were in the control room. "Thanks for staying," he said.

"I couldn't go. I feel responsible for this."

"Nonsense, you didn't throw the snake on me."

"I want to be here," Jade said.

"Well thank you. Under that hard shell of yours you can be really sweet."

"Thanks, but don't tell anyone," she said with a smile. "You should probably rest."

"I don't want to rest Jade. I'm afraid that if I close my eyes they'll never open again."

She reached down and held his hand. "You're going to be fine. I promise."

"After losing Steve, we can't lose William too," Michelle said.

"He's got a chance," Tom said. "Kiya and the others will give it their best shot. I just hope they get back in time."

5

O'Dell was keeping track of how long they were taking. They had reached the Dambroo village in one hour and fifty minutes. Kiya immediately led them to a small hut. Inside was a middle-aged man with brown hair. She introduced the man as Jango. Kiya and Jango continued talking in Dambroo.

"What's going on?" Sara asked Tabitha.

"I'm not sure, but I think she is asking him for his raft," Tabby answered.

When Kiya was done talking to Jango she said, "Dako."

"Sarto Kai," he replied. Kiya led them around back where there was a raft and two oars. It was only about eight feet long and four feet wide.

"We're not all going to fit on this," Sara said.

"I know," Kiya replied. They grabbed the raft and left the village. They began walking north. Michael checked his watch. They had been gone for two hours and ten minutes. They were behind schedule.

"We need to hurry," Michael said. "We are falling behind schedule." They all began to walk faster.

6

William was asleep now as Michelle walked over to Jade. "You like him don't you?" Michelle asked.

"Why do you care?" Jade replied.

"I just noticed that you have been spending a lot of time with him lately."

"He is the only person that understands me. I'm not in love or anything like that. It's just nice to have a friend."

"You would have a lot more if you gave the rest of us a chance," Michelle said.

"I can't deal with people, okay. People annoy me. You're not bad and O'Dell and Tabby are okay, but everyone else annoys me."

"Alright, I can see Sara, but what about the others?" Michelle asked. "How do they annoy you?"

"Forget it," Jade said. "I don't want to talk about it."

"Why not?" Michelle asked.

"They are your friends. I don't want to talk bad about them in front of you."

"Why don't you like Coy," Michelle asked.

"He's a nice guy," Jade said. "He's just stupid."

Michelle laughed a little bit. "He is kind of dumb."

"And Tom is nice. He just annoys me with all his scientific talk."

"That does get old," Michelle agreed.

"I hope he is going to be okay," Jade said as she looked down at William.

"What about Kiya?" Michelle asked.

"Huh?" Jade said confused.

"What bothers you about Kiya?"

"Oh," Jade said. "I don't know. There is just something about her I don't like. What about you?" Jade asked.

"What do you mean?" Michelle asked her.

"It must be tough for you. You know with Kiya. Tabby and you were so close. Now, Tabby spends all of her time with Kiya."

"Well I do miss talking to Tabby, but she is just trying to learn the Dambroo language."

"I wouldn't be so forgiving," Jade said.

"Do you think that maybe you're jealous of Kiya?" Michelle asked.

"Why would I be jealous of Kiya?" Jade snapped.

"Because you're no longer the only tough girl around. Kiya can take care of herself too."

"So," Jade said. "That's good. If she can take care of herself then it's one less person I have to worry about."

"That sounds good," Michelle said as she began to walk away, "but I don't believe that is how you actually feel."

7

O'Dell and the others were traveling at a good pace. Unfortunately traveling fast has its setbacks. They were startled by two Raptors that jumped out in front of them. O'Dell instantly shot one as the other crouched with its claws forward and let out a screech as it pounced. Kiya threw her spear hitting the creature in the throat. Its body landed on Tabitha, its intended lunch. The weight dropped her to the ground. She felt the beast's last warm breath exhale from its nostrils onto her face. Coy and Michael pulled the Velociraptor off of Tabby.

"Thanks," Tabby said. She walked over to Kiya and gave her a big hug. "You saved my life," she said.

"Welcome," Kiya replied.

"Let's go!" Michael said. "We have to save William's life." They continued on.

8

Jade knelt down beside William and put her hand on his forehead. He was burning up. She could feel the life slipping out of him. *'How much longer does he have?'* she thought. *'Not long. Please make it.'*

"How's he doing?" Michelle asked. Jade had a tear rolling down her cheek. She stood up and walked away. *'I guess he's not doing good,'* Michelle thought. She took Jade's place beside William while Jade gathered her emotions.

9

The others arrived at the lake. O'Dell checked his watch. They had been gone for six hours and five minutes. *'We're taking too long,"* he thought. The island was only about three hundred yards from shore. "Why did we need a raft?" Michael asked. "I could have swam that far."

"No," Kiya said. "Forsona doesn't bother raft. You swim, you supper."

"What's a Forsona?" Michael asked.

Kiya pointed to the left of the island. Michael looked to see a long neck sticking out of the water.

"Isn't that one of those Bronto things," Coy asked. "They don't eat us."

"It's not a Brontosaurus," Sara said. "Look at its head. It's a little narrower."

"Well we can't all fit on the raft so who's going?" Wesley asked.

"Kiya is the only one that knows what this plant looks like," Sara said.

"I go," Kiya agreed.

"I'll go too," Tabby added.

"Be quick," O'Dell said. "We're running out of time."

They got on the raft and began rowing out to the island.

10

Jade was back by William's side. She had a damp cloth on his forehead. She struggled to control her tears. William's eyes slowly opened. "You are beautiful," he said. "Thank you for being here with me."

Jade smiled as a tear ran down her cheek. "Rest," she insisted. William closed his eyes and went back to sleep.

11

Kiya and Tabitha had reached the island. Kiya ran over to a bunch of yellow flowers. They resembled daisies. She picked three and returned to the raft. They began to make their way back to shore as the others watched with interest.

"We're running out of time," Tabby said.

"I'll run the Sacharoo back to home," Kiya said.

When they got back to shore Michael looked at his watch. They had been gone for six hours and thirty minutes.

"I'll see you back at the ship," Kiya said as she ran off with the flowers.

"I hope she makes it," O'Dell said.

"Me too," Wesley agreed.

"I have never seen a flower like that before," Tabitha said. "It must be some form of hybrid or new species."

"Well I've never seen half the stuff I've seen here," Sara stated.

"Let's just hope it works," O'Dell said.

12

Back at the ship Tom and Michelle were talking. "How is he doing?" Tom asked.

"He is running a bad fever," Michelle answered.

"Is Jade still with him?" Tom asked.

"She hasn't left his side."

"I didn't see her as the caring type," Tom mentioned.

"Her and William have suddenly and surprisingly gotten close. I mean, if you were there in New York when we met Jade, she was really rude to William. He tried to ask her a few questions and she snapped at him. Now it seems as though they are best friends."

13

Meanwhile, Kiya was running through the jungle with her spear in one hand and the flowers in the other. She slowed down to a jog after about fifteen minutes. She entered a small clearing with fifteen Gallimimus in it. They ran off as she entered the forest on the other side of the clearing.

O'Dell and the others kept walking. "We should still pick up the pace," Michael said. "We don't want to be out here after dark."

"You're right," Tabby agreed. They began to walk faster. As they were walking they came across an Ankylosaurus. The beast stared at them with interest and let out a roar. Tabby must have ventured too close. The Ankylosaurus swung its massive clubbed tail at her. She immediately fell to the ground and watched the tail pass over her head. It struck a tree and made a thud. Loose branches and leaves fell to the ground. Tabitha got up and backed away from the beast. They walked around it and continued on.

14

Kiya entered the field and headed toward the ship. She had left the lake about two hours ago. She had made great time. She only hoped her prediction was right and that she had made it in time to save William. Michelle looked out to see Kiya running through the field with the flowers in hand. "Jade," Michelle said. "I've got good news." Jade looked over at Michelle. "Your flowers are here." Jades face brightened a little.

"The others are back this soon?" Tom asked.

"No," Michelle said. "Just Kiya."

Kiya entered the ship and walked over to William who had just awakened. His face was pale and he was drowsy. "Eat," Kiya said as she handed William a petal. He chewed it and swallowed with a disgusted look on his face. "You have to eat about four or five more," Kiya said.

"I think I'd rather die," William said.

"Eat up!" Jade snapped. William ate five more and then fell asleep. "Is he going to be okay?" Jade asked.

"We won't know until morning, but I think he's okay," Kiya said.

"Thank you," Jade said sincerely.

"Your welcome," she responded with a smile.

"Where are the others," Tom asked.

"I left them awhile ago. His chances were better that way. They should come around dark."

Jade lay down next to William and put her arm around him.

15

The others were slowly making their way through the forest. The long walk was tiring them. Michael and Coy each had a hand on the raft. Occasionally Wesley subbed in for one of them.

"It is going to get dark soon," Sara said.

"Yes," Michael agreed. "We must pick up the pace."

"We should leave the raft," Sara suggested. "It is only slowing us down."

"No," Tabitha snapped. She was normally quiet but this enraged her. "It's not ours to leave! Jango was nice enough to loan it to us. The least we could do is return it."

"She's right," O'Dell said. "If it weren't for Jango, William would have surely died."

"He might still die," Sara said.

Back at the ship Tom and Paul had turned in for the night. Jade was still with William. Kiya and Michelle waited up for the others. "They are couple?" Kiya asked as she pointed to Jade and William.

"Not that I know of," Michelle answered. "I guess that Jade just became close friends with him over the last couple days."

"They look like a couple," Kiya said.

It was dark as the others reached the field. "We made it," Sara said.

"Yeah, I wonder if William is alright," Tabby said.

"We'll take the raft back in the morning," O'Dell said. "Let's all get some rest."

They entered the ship and were greeted by Michelle and Kiya. "You're back," Michelle said as she hugged Tabitha.

"Where's mine," Wesley said. Michelle just smiled at him. "A brother can't get no play, damn!"

"How's William?" Tabby asked.

"We won't know until morning," Kiya answered.

Sara approached William's bed and snickered at the sight of Jade cuddling with him. She exited and joined the others. "That's cozy," she said as she pointed toward the bed.

"Let it be," Michelle said. "She's just worried about him."

"Yeah, well I'm worried about him too but I'm not in there draped all over him."

"Jealous?" Michelle asked.

Sara became enraged. "Jealous! No! Why would I be jealous of her? I could have him if I wanted."

"Knock it off girls," O'Dell said. "Let's get some sleep."

Sara glared at Michelle as she turned and walked away. Tabby walked up to Michelle. "She can be a bitch," Tabby said. "Don't let her bother you."

"I'm not bothered. She's just lucky Jade was sleeping. Jade would probably kick her ass for that."

"Come on," Tabby said. "Let's go to bed." Everyone turned in for the night.

16

The next morning Sara, Tom and Paul were up early. Tom and Paul were talking about the planet and where to explore next. Sara was stewing about Jade and William. Jade was awake in bed with William. She felt his head and was happy to find the fever had passed. William opened his eyes to see Jade smiling down at him. "You're okay," she said as she leaned forward and kissed his forehead.

"Oh please," Sara muttered under her breath. "What a skank," she said as she walked off. Everyone was awake now except Wesley. Tabitha, Michelle and Kiya were preparing to return the raft to Jango.

"How do you feel?" Jade asked William.

"I feel great," he said. "It was nice waking up next to you. We should try that again sometime."

"Maybe," Jade said with a smile. "But I don't think it will happen."

"Why not?" he asked.

"When you're too sick to move I have nothing to worry about. I'm not sure a healthy William would control himself and act like a gentleman." She got up and began to walk away.

"Where are you going?" he asked.

"I'm going with Tabby, Michelle, and Kiya to return the raft they used to get your medicine."

"Be careful," he said.

"Don't worry, I will." She turned and walked away.

Sara approached William's bed with a smile. "Hey Sara," he said.

"You're better," she said as she slowly leaned down and kissed him on the lips.

William was shocked and confused. "What was that for?"

"I'm just glad you're alright. I wouldn't want to lose you."

'What did I miss,' he thought. *'How long have I been out. First Jade is cuddling with me. Now Sara is kissing me.'*

Chapter Eleven:
The Pocala

1

Jade, Michelle, Kiya, and Tabitha were on their way to the Dambroo village with the raft. They were taking turns carrying it. Jade and Michelle had it at this point.

"So," Tabby said to Jade. "William's snake bite really brought you two together."

"We're not together," Jade quickly replied.

"I mean close," Tabby corrected herself.

"Yeah, I guess so," Jade admitted. "We've just become good friends."

"Jade," Michelle said. "Be careful about Sara."

"What do you mean?" Jade inquired.

"She acted really jealous last night when she saw the two of you together."

"Why? Sara doesn't want William."

"Well, she said that she could have him if she wanted to," Michelle added.

"That bitch," Jade said.

"I thought you two weren't a couple?" Tabitha asked.

"We're not. But he doesn't need to be hurt by that little snot. She's just using him to piss me off. We need to hurry and get back before she gets her claws in him."

2

Tom, Paul, Coy, and O'Dell went hunting with spears. They wanted the practice, plus had a limited supply of bullets left for the gun. "Do you think the girls will be alright?" Tom asked.

"They'll be fine," O'Dell answered. "Jade and Kiya can fight with the best of them."

"Hey look," Coy whispered as he pointed. There was a deer about thirty feet away.

"Go ahead," O'Dell said.

"No," Coy answered. "You do it Mike. You have the best aim." Michael took about four steps forward and launched his spear. It landed just over the deer. The deer quickly ran off.

"Oh well," Paul said. "I'm sure something will come along."

Just then a Raptor leaped out from the bushes. It was staring at Coy who was frozen with fear in front of it. Tom threw his spear and hit the Raptor in the shoulder. The spear did minimal damage and fell out. The Raptor glanced over at Tom then returned its focus to Coy. Paul launched his spear and hit the Raptor in the stomach. The spear stuck as blood ran down from the wound. The Raptor knocked the spear out with its hand and glared at Paul. Then it pounced on Coy who fell to the ground with his spear up. The spear impaled the Raptor but the creature managed to sink its dewclaw into Coy's hip.

The Raptor died on top of Coy. He felt the warm blood pouring down on him.

"Are you okay?" Tom asked.

"It got me pretty good," Coy said. "But I'll live." Coy pushed the Raptor off of him.

"What the hell were we thinking," O'Dell said. "From now on we bring the gun for protection."

"Yes," Tom agreed. "We mustn't get over confident out here. There are just too many ways to die." They got out a Machete and began to cut the Raptor up.

3

William didn't know why Sara kissed him. Was it because she liked him or because she was happy he was okay. He got up and began to walk away from Sara and his cot. She grabbed his arm.

"Where are you going?" she asked.

"I was going to go start a fire," he answered.

"We'll have time to do that later. Sit with me," she said. He sat down with a puzzled look on his face. "So why is Jade stringing you along?" Sara asked. "She doesn't want you. She won't go any farther than a kiss. She is just using you."

"What on Earth would she be using me for?" he asked.

"We're not on Earth sweetie," Sara said with a smile. "I don't know what she'd be using you for but she doesn't love you."

"We are just friends," William explained.

"Has she ever kissed you on the lips?" Sara asked.

"Yes, once. But that…"

Sara immediately kissed William on the lips. "I'm your friend too. If she can kiss you so can I."

"I'm not complaining," William said lightly.

"I care about you more than she does so I should be able to do more than just kiss you." She put her arms around him and they locked in a longer more passionate kiss.

4

The girls had reached the Dambroo village. They returned the raft and oars to Jango and expressed their gratitude.

"Come on," Jade said. "We have to hurry back before that little bitch seduces William."

"Why do you even care?" Tabitha asked. "You two aren't a couple. If she wants him, let her have him. He can make his own decisions."

"She doesn't want him though," Jade said. "She just wants to play with his emotions."

"What do you think you're doing?" Tabitha asked.

"I'm not leading him on!" Jade snapped.

"Oh, so you like him?" Tabby asked.

"Well, no."

"Then you're leading him on because he obviously likes you."

"I'm not trying to lead him on," Jade said. Suddenly Jade felt a blow to the back of her neck and she was out cold. Kiya and Tabitha turned to see five men attacking them. Michelle was screaming as two of them left with her in their possession. Tabitha and Kiya were about to attack the men in front of them when they each felt blows to the back of their heads. The butt end of the men's spears hit them. They had been surrounded and ambushed. Everything went black as Tabby and Kiya were out as well.

5

Meanwhile, Sara and William were getting quite comfortable. Sara pulled William's shirt off. She began kissing him and sucking on his neck. She straddled him on the bed and began kissing his neck and continued lower. She reached his bellybutton when they heard O'Dell from the other room.

"We need a bandage for Coy," he said. "He's hurt pretty bad."

Sara got up and smiled at William. "I guess we'll have to continue this later," she said.

"Yeah," he panted. "I guess so."

Sara went and got a bandage for Coy from the med-kit while William put his shirt back on. Tom started a fire and began to cook the cut up Raptor while everyone waited for the girls to return from the Dambroo village.

6

Jade awoke to see Kiya and Tabitha out cold next to her. Michelle was nowhere to be found. Jade stumbled to her feet with a headache. She shook Tabby a little to wake her. "Wake up," Jade said. Tabitha woke with a groan. Her head was also aching. Kiya woke and sat up next to them. They helped each other up.

"Who were those men?" Jade asked.

"Pocala," Kiya answered. "They have killed many of my people."

"Why didn't they kill us?" Tabby asked.

"They didn't need us," Kiya answered, "just Michelle."

"Why did they need Michelle?" Jade asked.

"Every time the large morning star gets its brightest, they sacrifice one person to the creature to make it happy. The creature sends the star away so it doesn't get too close to them. They believe the star will melt them if they don't make the creature happy. If they don't sacrifice someone the creature will get mad and destroy them all. This is what they believe. Our people have tried to reason with them but they won't listen. When we sent a group to talk to them they held the entire group hostage and sent them all to the creature one by one."

"They are going to sacrifice Michelle?" Tabby asked. "We have to save her!"

"We must get the others and the gun," Kiya said. "It is our only hope. We have time, they won't sacrifice her until tomorrow night."

They began to walk back to the ship.

"Do you know where they are taking her?" Jade asked.

"Yes," Kiya answered. "Their village is past the Guanco Jaballa. You would call it the Great Desert."

7

Back at camp Coy was resting his hip while Tom continued cooking the Raptor. Sara was sitting next to

William by the fire. "Were you having fun?" she asked with a smile.

"Yeah, I guess," he answered.

"You guess!" she said angrily. "You're telling me that you're not even interested in me?"

"No that's not what I mean. I'm interested, but I … I don't know."

"You don't know what?" she asked as they stood up.

"I like Jade too," he said.

"So what?" Sara said. "The difference is that Jade doesn't like you! I can make you happy."

"I'm not so sure that Jade doesn't like me," he said. "She seems interested at times."

"Jade would only use you."

William began to walk away. Sara grabbed his arm and spun him around to face her. "Jade can't make you feel as good as I can. That is a fact!" Sara said as she turned and walked away.

Tom was concentrating on the Raptor and didn't hear any of this from the other side of the fire pit. He saw Jade, Kiya, and Tabby sprinting across the field toward him. He yelled inside for the others to join him. Everyone came out as the girls reached the ship. "Get the tents, and gun," Jade said. "We have to rescue Michelle."

"Where is she?" Tom asked.

"The Pocala took her," Kiya said. "They will sacrifice her tomorrow night. We need to go save her."

Everyone gathered their spears, the gun and two tents. "Coy, you should stay here," O'Dell said.

"I can make it," he said. "I want to help."

"You smell of blood," Kiya said. "You will lead Raptors right to us."

"She's right," Paul said. "I'll stay here with you."

"I'll stay too," Tom said. "I would only slow you down. Michelle is like a daughter to me, please save her."

"We'll do our best," O'Dell said.

8

They began to walk toward the east. Michael and Kiya led the way followed by Tabby and Wesley. Sara, William, and Jade brought up the rear. Jade slowed her pace when they reached the woods. She pulled William back with her. The others were in clear view, but far enough away not to hear her.

"So how was your day with Sara?" she asked.

"It was okay. Why?" William asked.

"Just okay? I'll bet she made it more than just okay."

"What do you care?" he asked.

"She doesn't like you William."

"She seemed to like me just fine earlier," he replied.

"She's just using you to piss me off!" Jade said angrily.

"Sounds like it's working," he replied.

"Well, do you like her?" Jade asked.

"She was certainly fun to be around," he replied. "Why do you think she is using me? Is it that hard to believe that I can get an attractive girl?"

"William," she said calmly. "Of course you can get an attractive girl. You're a good-looking, nice guy. But, Sara doesn't want you."

"What about you?" he asked.

Jade rolled her eyes at the thought of answering this question; she knew that it would come up sooner or later.

"I think you're great, but I'm not looking for a guy right now."

"Then why do you care if I'm with Sara?"

"You won't be with Sara," Jade explained. "She is using you to make me mad. I care because I don't want you to get hurt."

Sara had noticed they dropped back and quickly came back to join them. "Spending a lot of time back here," she said. "Not trying to steal my man are you Jade?"

Jade became furious. "He's not your man and I'm not like you. If I wanted to take your man I wouldn't have to seduce him. I'd just kick your little Shirley Temple carrot-top ass!"

"Now, now," Sara kidded. "Violence is never the answer. Besides, I'm a lover not a fighter."

"Yeah, you love yourself," Jade replied.

"William, don't waste your time with Jade. She bats for the home team. She likes women."

"Fuck you!" Jade said as she shoved Sara to the ground.

Sara got back up and walked over to William and cupped her hand on the side of his face. "You can choose sweetie," she said. "She's good at dishing out pain, but I'm the one who can give you endless pleasure."

"Yeah, and herpes," Jade added.

"Knock it off," William interjected. "You both seem to be good at arguing and I'm not sure that I want to deal with that right now." He increased his pace and caught up with the others. Sara gave Jade a piercing stare as they did the same.

9

Tom, Paul, and Coy were sitting by the fire. "You could have gone," Coy said. "I'll be fine."

"We would have slowed them down," Paul commented.

"Yes, they have a better chance without us," Tom added.

"I know Michelle is like a daughter to you Tom," Coy said. "Don't worry, they'll save her."

"I hope so," Tom said.

"Listen Tom," Coy said. "Michael is as good as it gets at this type of thing. He does it for a living. Jade can kick just about anyone's but. And Kiya knows this place better than anyone. Michelle will be fine."

"Thanks Coy," Simonson replied. Tom knew that Coy was right. He couldn't have designed a better group of people to rescue Michelle.

10

Meanwhile, Michelle was being led through the desert by the Pocala. She could try to escape but feared they would kill her. There were five of them and only one of her. The men stopped and were chattering quite a bit. It was a language different than Kiya's. She didn't understand them, but they seemed quite alarmed. Then she saw what they were startled by. There was a giant scorpion approaching ahead of them. Two of the men grabbed Michelle by the arms to secure her. The other three stood ahead with their spears in front of them. It approached them and attacked. It missed with its tail and created a cloud of dust from driving its tail into the sand. One of the men speared the creature in the side. The scorpion reached back with its pincher and snapped the spear out. Then it retaliated by driving its tail down into the man's chest. Blood squirted out as the man dropped. A second tribesman stabbed at it with his spear but missed. The scorpion removed his head with one of its large pinchers. Michelle turned away. She knew it was her chance to escape but she couldn't wiggle herself from their grasp. Plus they seemed to be doing everything in their power to protect her. The third Pocala stabbed the scorpion in the head. It let out a squeal and snapped the spear off. It was enough to detour the beast though, as it ran off. Michelle noticed a tear running down the tribesman's cheek as he knelt by one of the deceased men. They grieved for a moment then continued on through the desert.

11

Michael and the others had reached the desert now. They were well behind Michelle and the Pocala though. They continued through the desert for two hours before it started to get dark. "Let's make camp," O'Dell said. Michael and Tabby set up one tent while Wesley and William set up the other. Kiya watched with interest. She had never seen dwellings like these before.

12

The Pocala and Michelle had reached the end of the desert. They entered some rocky barren plains. Michelle was wondering where they were going and what they wanted with her. The men were different from the cannibals. They resembled the Dambroo people more closely. They had pale skin and were relatively clothed. The men were shirtless but wore a fur skirt of sorts. They continued to walk through the darkness for another two hours.

They finally arrived at a great wall of rocks. It had an opening about twelve feet wide. The Pocala led Michelle through the opening and into their village. There were several people who had gathered by the opening. They cheered as Michelle entered at spear-point. Men predominantly inhabited the village. There were a few women, but men definitely had the numbers.

A man came over with a grin on his face. He seemed to be in charge, possibly the chief. He was accompanied by two guards. He mumbled something in his language and pointed to the left. Michelle was then led in that direction to a large pit. It was about twenty feet deep, fifty feet long, and twenty feet wide. On one side of the pit were two poles with ropes on them. On the other side was a cave entrance. The cave was completely dark. Three men lowered a wooden staircase into the pit using some form of pulley system. Michelle was led into the pit. The two guards held her tight, one on each side of her. Michelle watched as a warrior from above raised a blowgun. He shot and hit Michelle in the neck. The dart stung like a bumblebee. She was beginning to become tired as she looked up at the star filled sky. The twinkling stars were the last things she saw.

13

The tents were up and everyone prepared for sleep. O'Dell, Wesley, and Tabby were in one tent. Kiya, Sara, William, and Jade were in the other. Kiya was fast asleep. Sara and Jade were on each side of William. William was pretending to sleep as he heard Jade and Sara whispering to each other.

"So why are you using him to piss me off?" Jade asked. "If you have a problem with me, see me about it."

"Who says I'm using him?" Sara responded. "Maybe I like him. I'm just trying to show him that you're not the only option." William continued to listen to the whispering catfight with interest.

"I never even said that I was an option," Jade stated. "I guess the option to have you, however, is always open just like your legs."

"I'm sorry," Sara remarked snottily. "You're not an option because, number one; I'm better, and number two; you prefer women."

"I don't prefer women!" Jade said as her voice became a little louder. She grabbed William and planted a kiss on him. He pretended to be awoken and startled which wasn't hard because he was startled. Then, Sara grabbed him and also planted a kiss on him.

"Hey," he said. "Do I get a say in this?"

"No!" they both said simultaneously. Kiya was starting to toss at the increased volume in the tent. Jade looked over at Sara and held her finger to her lips. Sara nodded.

The one thing they did agree on was that this was their problem and did not want to include the others. They both went outside and left William in the tent with Kiya. The sky was filled with stars.

"Why do you pretend to want him just to piss me off?" Jade asked.

"I'm not pretending," Sara responded. "I do want him."

"You don't love him!" Jade argued.

Sara smiled devilishly at her. "Maybe not," she said. "But we've been out here for twenty-four days now. Not to mention the long ass time on the ship getting here. I deserve to have a little fun."

"Not at his expense!" Jade said as she approached Sara.

"I look out for myself," Sara replied. "That is how I do things." Jade just glared at Sara who was still smiling. "Oh don't worry," Sara said. "William will get lots of pleasure out of this."

"I won't let you do this," Jade said.

"You can't stop me," Sara said confidently. "If he wants me there is nothing you can do."

"You're a bitch!" Jade said.

Sara reacted with a right hook that connected with Jade's cheek. The punch snapped Jade's head backwards. Jade retaliated with a spinning roundhouse kick that hit Sara's jaw, sending her to the sand. Jade hopped on top of her and began punching. William heard the scuffle and ran outside. He tackled Jade off of Sara.

"Knock it off you two!" he whisper-yelled. "When we started this mission, neither of you were interested in me. I'm not sure that you like me now. You just hate each other so much that you want something to fight over. I want nothing to do with either of you until you can start getting along." He angrily walked back into the tent.

"You didn't have to keep hitting me," Sara said.

"You started it," Jade replied. "I wasn't going to touch you, but when you punched me I changed my mind."

"It was a good punch though wasn't it?" Sara asked with a smile as she lay on the sand.

"Yeah, not bad," Jade said as she felt the side of her face. "I have to admit, you've got guts. Nobody has ever picked a fight with me before."

"Don't get used to it. I'm done. I see why you're the champ." Sara paused for a moment. "No, actually I feel why you're the champ."

Jade walked over to Sara and helped her up. They entered the tent to see William lying next to Kiya.

"So who sleeps next to him?" Sara asked.

"I do of course," Jade replied. "You were on the outside."

William lightly shook Kiya and whispered something in her ear. Kiya then rolled up on top of William, and then rolled off the other side. Now William was by the wall of the tent. William leaned over and kissed Kiya on the cheek. "Thank you," he said.

"Well that's bullshit," Sara whispered to Jade.

"So," Jade said light heartedly. "Wanna fight over who sleeps next to Kiya?"

"No, you can have that one," Sara replied. They lay down and went to sleep.

14

The next morning, Michelle awoke in the pit. She was completely naked with her arms and legs spread and tied to the poles. The Pocala continued on with their daily duties, ignoring Michelle. Many thoughts began to enter Michelle's head a she began to panic. *'What are they planning for me?'* she wondered. *'Are the others coming to help me? Do they even know where I am?'* She felt hopeless.

15

O'Dell woke everyone up as they continued to pursue the Pocala. William walked next to Kiya and avoided Sara and Jade all morning. They walked behind Kiya and William. William kept the distance enough so he wouldn't have to hear them and vice versa. "So how do you like it here?" he asked Kiya.

"It's my home," Kiya answered. "I guess I like it fine." She glanced over at William with an inquiring look. "Who do you care for?" she asked. "Sara or Jade?"

"Both I guess," William answered. "But neither right now."

"Well I really don't want to get involved," Kiya said. "I feel that talking to you makes them both hate me."

"Oh don't worry," William assured her. "They're not going to hate you."

"I hate her," Sara said to Jade.

Jade smiled, "Is there anyone you like?"

"Of course," Sara said. "Myself," she said with a grin. Jade and Sara exchanged a light laugh.

They approached the bodies of the Pocala that the scorpion dispensed of.

"Keep your eyes open," O'Dell said.

"Do you think Michelle is alright?" Tabby asked.

"I think there is a good chance. I don't see her body," O'Dell said.

"Well at least we know that we're on the right track," Jade said. They continued through the desert.

16

Back at the ship Coy, Paul, and Tom were outside around the fire pit.

"How's your hip?" Simonson asked.

"It's okay. I think I should walk on it for a while."

"Good," Tom said. "What do you say we try out this fishing net that we got from the Dambroo?"

"I'm game," Coy answered.

"If you don't mind I'd like to stay here in case the others return," Paul said.

Coy and Tom agreed and they began to walk to the creek. "Tom, I just wanted to thank you for inviting me on this adventure," Coy said as they walked.

"Don't thank me, thank Sara. She made the decision for you to come along, I merely suggested it."

"Yeah, but I wouldn't be here if it weren't for you, so thanks."

"Don't sell yourself short son," Tom said. "If it weren't for you fixing the ship, none of us would be here."

"I guess your right," Coy agreed.

17

The others had reached the end of the desert and began walking across the rocky plains. Jade pulled William aside. "I'm sorry," she said. "I was only looking out for your best interest."

"How about you let me handle that," William said.

"She doesn't care about you," Jade added.

"So. Do you? I never know what I'm getting with you. At least Sara is straight forward."

"There is a difference between straight forward and easy. She is just trying to sleep with you."

"I know that, but you don't show any interest in me so why do you care?"

Jade grabbed him and kissed him. "I'm interested," she said with cute puppy dog eyes. "I just control myself because I'm not a slut."

"Promise me that you'll be honest with me and won't hold your feelings back," William demanded.

"I'll try," Jade answered. "That is something that is really hard for me. I can be honest, that is no problem. I have trouble showing how I feel though. I promise that I'll try William."

"Good, I'll avoid Sara for awhile. But let me handle her," he said sternly. "You don't need to be starting fights with her."

"Fine," Jade agreed.

18

Back at the stream, Coy scooped the net out of the water. "Two more!" he said as he threw them in the pail with the others. Tom was distant. Coy could see something was bothering him. "What's wrong?" Coy asked.

"I just hope that Michelle is alright. I'm the one who suggested her to Sara. I just thought she could use a vacation from her job. She works so hard. I never meant to put her in danger."

"Professor, don't worry. The others will save her. Don't blame yourself. We all knew that there was danger involved in this mission. She is here because she wants to be, not because of you."

"Thank you Coy, you are a good man."

19

The others had reached the Pocala village. They quietly entered through the opening in the wall and snuck behind one of the stone houses.

"Over there," Kiya said as she pointed to the pit. They were too far away to see down into the entrance. They snuck up and hid behind a closer house. There was chanting coming from the pit. The tribesmen were too engulfed in their ritual to notice the explorers. The explorers stepped to the edge of the pit so they could see.

"She's naked," O'Dell commented.

"Yes, it is part of the celebration," Kiya explained.

"She's pretty hot," William joked as he took a slight elbow in the gut from Jade.

"Pretty hot?" Wesley asked. "She is fine!"

"We're here to save her, not gawk!" Jade said.

Two of the Pocala had a subdued deer that they held in front of Michelle. It must have been drugged or something. It was clearly alive but didn't struggle from their grasp. They slit its throat and blood sprayed everywhere. The chief gathered as much blood as he could with his hands. He began to smear the blood all over Michelle with his hands. Michelle squirmed in protest but the poles held her firm.

"What is he doing?" William asked.

"He is marking her for the beast. This way the beast knows who the sacrifice is.

"We have to act now," O'Dell said. Although the pit was filled with about twenty-five Pocala, only about ten were armed guards. The rest were ordinary citizens.

"Okay," Michael said. "William, Kiya and I will go down and save Michelle. The four of you need to stay up here in case we need you."

Michael, William, and Kiya walked down the wooden stairs while Jade, Sara, Wesley, and Tabby stayed on top of the pit. Michael carried his gun while William and Kiya each had spears. When they reached the bottom of the pit they were noticed. The Pocala guards raised their spears while the citizens appeared to be a little scared.

"Kiya, do you know their language?" Michael asked.

"Not really," she answered. "I know a little bit." Michael began to approach the chief with his gun raised. The chief motioned and one of the guards charged with spear in hand. Michael turned and shot the guard in the chest, killing him. Then he turned back toward the chief. The Pocala citizens were definitely panicked now. They all scrambled to the stairs as the guards held firm in their positions. The citizens ran out of the pit and stayed clear of Wesley, Sara, and Jade. They stayed near and watched though. The chief sent two more guards after O'Dell. He shot both of them. Now the remaining guards and chief sprinted past O'Dell and headed up the stairs. Michael ran over to Michelle.

"Thank God!" she said.

"Are you ready to leave?" he asked. "Or has this place grown on you."

"I'm ready, trust me," she said as he untied her. Her body was covered in blood. There were smeared handprints all over her.

"Why did they give up so easily?" Michelle asked.

"They must have been scared of the gun," O'Dell answered.

"Run!" William yelled to them.

O'Dell turned to see the beast emerging from the cave. "Maybe it wasn't the gun," he said. The beast was enormous. It walked on four legs and had a fin on its back twenty feet high. The creature was the length of a bus.

"It looks like some form of Edaphasaurus or Dimetrodon, but it's huge compared to them," Michelle said as they ran toward the stairs with the others. Unfortunately the stairs were being raised.

"The beast comes out for the sun and to feed," Kiya explained. "That is why they sacrifice on this day. The sun is closest."

They turned and faced the beast with their backs to the wall. O'Dell raised his gun.

"There is no way you're going to kill it," Michelle said.

"I can slow it down," he said as he fired. The bullet tore a small hole into the beast's leg. The creature seemed unfazed by the bullet. Suddenly, the stairs lowered back down.

They ran up the stairs to see the chief being held hostage at Jade's knifepoint. William looked around to find some water for Michelle. There was a man outside of his house with a pail of water in hand. William walked over to him and the man dropped the bucket and ran inside. William grabbed it and walked over to Michelle. "I wouldn't want you attracting Raptors as well as men with your body," he said lightly. Jade looked over with a disapproving glare. Michelle lightly chuckled as her face was slightly red from embarrassment and slightly stained from blood. Jade was still holding the chief hostage. In the pit, the creature feasted on the deer carcass.

A female citizen approached William and Michelle. She was carrying Michelle's clothes. She had a sympathetic look on her face as she handed Michelle the clothes. "Thank you," Michelle said with a smile. After what these people had done to her she still managed to smile at this lady. Michelle was a complex person. She was very modest and humble. She understood civilizations and how hierarchy and religion worked. She knew that this lady had only gone along with what her people had always believed in. Michelle got dressed and they all headed toward the opening of the village wall. When they arrived, Jade released the chief and the explorers headed toward the desert.

"Thanks for saving me," Michelle said.

"Thank you!" William joked.

'Grow up,' Jade thought as jealousy began to fill her.

Sara approached William who tried to look away. "You think her body is nice?" she asked. "You should see mine baby." Then, she smiled and walked away.

20

Coy, Paul, and Tom sat by the fire eating fish. "The others should be back tomorrow if they were successful," Paul said.

"Yes," Tom said. "Let's hope they were successful."

They were interrupted by two Gallimimus sprinting across the field in front of them. "We should get inside," Tom said. "They are being chased."

"Yes," Paul agreed. "And we don't want to deter whatever is chasing them." They quickly ran into the ship and peered outside. Three Raptors broke free from the covering of the forest and entered the field in chase of the Gallimimus. The chase ended by the ships door. One of the Gallimimus tripped on a bucket and fell to the ground. A Raptor drove its claw down into it as the other two joined it. They feasted by the ship door until dusk. After the Raptors left, Tom, Paul, and Coy went outside.

"I think we should move the carcass so we don't draw scavengers," Paul said.

"I agree," Simonson added. The three of them dragged the remains quite far into the woods before returning to the ship and going to bed.

21

"Let's make camp and return in the morning," O'Dell said. They set up the tents in the desert sand. O'Dell, Tabby, Wesley, and Kiya slept in one tent while the other was being stabilized. When it was finished, William grabbed a spot by the wall. Jade went in and cuddled with him. Sara was put off by this and stayed outside for a while. Michelle slept on the other side of Jade. An hour later, Sara came in and went to sleep.

They slept uninterrupted until O'Dell woke them all in the morning. They continued through the desert with no signs of giant scorpions and entered the woods. After an uninterrupted trip through the forest they entered the field to the ship.

"Home," Michelle said. "I didn't think I would ever see it again."

Tom was walking through the field to greet them with a large smile. He hugged Michelle with all his might. "I'm so glad you're okay," he said. "Thank you all for saving her."

Coy and Paul joined them.

"She is like family to me too Tom," Tabby said. "I would have done anything to save her."

"You're all like family to me," Kiya added.

"Hey Coy," William said. "You missed out. Michelle took her clothes off for us."

Michelle gave William a friendly shove as Jade walked off. Things were back to normal for the next couple of days; as normal as it gets on a planet of dinosaurs, cannibals, and apemen.

Chapter Twelve:
The Collector

1

The explorers woke to a warm sunny day. They were low on water but nobody really wanted to make the long trek through the forest. They decided to draw sticks. The two shortest sticks would fetch the water. William grabbed eleven sticks and held them in his hand. Coy drew first and had a modest stick. Tom was and Paul drew next. Both of their sticks were longer than Coy's. Wesley drew a stick shorter than Coy's. O'Dell drew a long stick. Sara was next. Her stick was by far the shortest. As of right now it was Sara and Wesley going for water. Michelle, Tabby, and Kiya drew long sticks. It was just Jade and William left. Jade pulled one of the two remaining sticks. It was a little larger than Sara's. Wesley was off the hook. William opened his hand and revealed another small stick. He held it up to Jade's. Jade's was shorter.

"God damn it," she mumbled. She was a little bummed about getting the water but realized that it would be better because at least Sara and William wouldn't be alone.

"Super!" Sara said sarcastically. "Let's go sweetheart." Jade grabbed a pail and rolled her eyes as they left. Sara carried a spear and Jade only had her knife.

"Boy that ought to be interesting," Michelle said.

"Oh well," William added. "They deserve to spend some time together."

2

Jade and Sara entered the forest. Sara had an annoying smile on her face while Jade had an angry glare. "Don't say anything and don't look at me and we'll be fine," Jade suggested.

"Don't look at you?" Sara asked. "You're the one who's always undressing me with your eyes. I know I'm hot but you can't have me."

"I'm not a fucking dyke!" Jade yelled.

"I know," Sara said calmly. "I just like messing with you."

"Well I love kicking your ass, so don't give me an excuse to!"

"There you go again," Sara said. "You're so manly. Don't you see? William doesn't want a man. He wants a woman. You have to be gentle and sexy not rough and tough."

"I can be. But right now I don't want to be."

"What is your problem with me?" Sara asked.

"Your snotty, and you tried to seduce William just because you dislike me," Jade answered.

"I'm not snotty," Sara said. "And so what if I dislike you. I have a right to my opinion."

"Why did you drag me along on this mission then?" Jade asked. "You chose me. I didn't choose to come. Why?"

Sara's mood quickly changed from joking and annoying to serious and somber. "When I saw you fighting I was like 'wow this girl can kick some ass.' You seemed cool. You seemed like someone that I would want as a friend. But you gave me the cold shoulder from the start."

"You don't need me as a friend," Jade said. "You've got lots of money. I'm sure friends flock to you."

"No, people flock to me," Sara said. "A friend is someone who could care less whether or not I have money."

"Oh yeah," Jade said. "I could care less about your stupid money and I'm not your friend."

"See that's where you're wrong," Sara explained. "You do care that I have money. It bothers you. That is why you didn't even give me a chance."

"Alright," Jade said. "I'll make you a deal. Leave William alone and I'll forget about our past and start over."

"I'll try," Sara said. They filled their pails with water and started to return home.

3

Back at the ship Michelle and William were sitting by the fire pit while Tabby was standing nearby

"So Michelle, could I see that nice body of yours again?" he asked.

"Sure," she said. "Maybe tonight. You can go to your bed and get ready for me. When you fall asleep maybe you'll see it in your dreams." She stood up and walked away and Tabby joined her.

'Ouch,' William thought. *'I guess I deserve that.'*

"That was pretty harsh," Tabby said.

"Yeah," Michelle agreed. "But I don't need to be in the middle of the Sara and Jade thing. He's already got two women fighting over him, I don't want any part of that."

Sara and Jade were returning with the water when they noticed two cannibals standing in front of them. They let the buckets down as the cannibals charged. Sara speared a cannibal in the chest as Jade threw her knife and impaled the other one's throat. Sara turned and thrust her spear at Jade. Jade dove out of the way as the spear impaled a third cannibal that was attacking from behind. Jade looked up at Sara from the ground. "What are you, fucking crazy?" she asked.

"You're welcome," Sara said calmly.

"You're welcome? You could have impaled me! How did you know I would move?"

"You're a fighter," Sara said. "It's your job to dodge. I watched you in all those matches. You were fighting the best in the world and barely got hit. It's your strategy to dodge. Good strategy because when I slugged you I almost knocked you on your ass."

"Don't get too cocky or I'll grant you a rematch," Jade said as Sara helped her up. "Thanks Sara. I didn't see that one coming so I guess you did kind of save me."

"One bite of you and they would have spit you out anyway," Sara commented. "Let's go home," she said as they grabbed their water.

4

Coy was outside by the fire pit as a large shadow covered him. He looked up to see a ship fly slowly over the field. This ship was larger than theirs. He ran inside and grabbed Simonson and O'Dell. They looked up just in time to see the ship descend below the tree line. Sara and Jade were running through the field toward them. "Did you see that?" Sara asked.

"I saw our way out of here," O'Dell added.

They went inside and called a meeting. They told the others about the ship "We should send an expedition to make contact with the ship's crew," Tom said. "Who wants to be a part of it?"

"I want to stay and pack," William said.

"I'll go," Michelle said. Kiya agreed to go with her.

"Don't you want to go back to your village and get your belongings?" William asked.

"Why?" Kiya answered. "I'm staying here. This is my home."

"But this place is so much more violent than our world," William explained.

"Is it?" Kiya asked. "Before you landed I had never seen a gun. At least here I know what I'm up against. I could never adjust to your world. It is best for me to stay here."

"I'll go with you two," Tabby said. They headed east in the direction of the crash.

"Well, if we're going home, I want some proof of this place's existence," Tom said.

"What do you mean?" William said. I still have the film.

"The film that we're unsure will develop properly?" Tom asked. "Even if it does turn out, people won't believe it is real. I want to bring back a dinosaur egg."

"You're crazy!" William said.

"No, he's right," Jade said. "I don't want to have come on this mission for no reason. We need proof."

5

Tom grabbed a backpack. He, Paul, Coy, Michael, Wesley, and Jade went in search of a dinosaur egg. Sara and William stayed behind and packed.

Tom and the others headed in the direction of the swamp where they saw the Hadrosaur eggs when they first arrived. O'Dell had the gun because their task would not be easy. Hadrosaurs were good mothers and never strayed far from the nest. When they arrived at the nest there were no eggs. Instead there were baby Hadrosaurs standing in and around the nest. They were very cute, but not what they needed.

"It's okay," Jade said. "I know where there is a Gallimimus nest. William and I came across it one day when we were getting water."

"Lead the way," Tom said. They began to head toward the stream.

6

William and Sara were packing as much as they could.

"So," William said, "We're alone."

"Yeah, I guess so," Sara said.

William walked over to her. "Aren't you going to kiss me or seduce me?" he asked.

"No, suddenly I'm not interested," she answered.

'What the hell is going on?' he thought. *'Am I going to end up with one of these girls or are they both playing me.'*

Sara began to pack her things as William approached her again.

"So you no longer like me?" he asked.

"That's not it," Sara said. "I just don't think that it's the appropriate time. We might be going home today."

William shrugged. "Yeah, I guess so," he said unenthusiastically.

"You don't want to go home?" Sara asked.

"Of course I do. Back home I don't get as many chances with women that's all. Out here I am spending a lot of time with several beautiful, intelligent women. Back home I wouldn't stand a chance with you or Jade."

"William," Sara said as she put her hand on his shoulder. "You're a great guy. You'll find a nice girl soon. I'm sure of it. Now, can we finish packing."

William smiled and nodded as they continued to pack.

7

Jade had led the others to the Gallimimus nest. There was no danger in sight. Tom walked over to the nest and grabbed a healthy egg. He carefully placed it in the backpack. "Now let's meet up with the girls to see who was flying our visiting ship," he said.

Kiya, Michelle, and Tabitha had arrived at the Great Desert. A few hundred feet away they could see the large ship. They walked through the desert toward the ship. When they were a few feet away the large door lowered. A well-built man wearing all black approached them. His face was the only uncovered part of his body. The skin was black around his eyes and gray everywhere else.

"Kai," the man said. Tabby was shocked and looked over to Kiya after she recognized this as a Dambroo greeting. She received no comfort from Kiya who had an equal look of shock. Kiya began to talk to the odd man in Dambroo.

"Who are you?" she asked.

"Arnemore," the man said.

"How do you know my language?"

"I have studied your people for many years," he answered in Dambroo. "They are an inspiration."

Tabitha introduced herself in Dambroo. Arnemore stepped back startled. "You are not Dambroo," he said. "There are no dark Dambroo."

"I know," Tabitha answered as the conversation continued in Dambroo. "I learned their language."

"What are you then?" he asked.

"American," she said.

"Another planet?" he asked in Dambroo. Tabby looked to Kiya because she didn't understand.

"Yes," Kiya answered him.

"Nice, very nice," he said.

"What's going on?" Michelle asked Kiya. "Do you know him?"

"No," Kiya answered. "I'm not sure I trust him either."

Tabitha asked Arnemore if he could give them a ride home or spare some fuel.

"I would love to," he said. "Come on in. But I must insist that you leave your spears outside. I am a peaceful man and want nothing to do with weapons."

"Well, we actually have some friends that need a ride also," Tabby said.

"That's okay," he said. "We can wait for them inside."

Kiya looked over to Michelle. "I don't like this," she said in English.

"Relax," Tabby said. "He's going to give us a ride back to Earth." Against Kiya's wishes they sat their spears down and entered the ship. The room inside was huge. It had some form of tiled floor. Each square tile was about five feet wide. There were gaps between the tiles and each one had some form of lettering on it. There was a large control panel on one side of the room. Arnemore was headed toward the control panel. He started the ship and shut the door.

"We must wait for our friends," Tabby said.

"I am," replied Arnemore. "I just wanted to warm the ship up."

He quickly pressed three buttons. Cages rose from the gaps of the tiles they were on. Kiya leaped over hers and rolled on the ground. Tabby and Michelle were trapped as the cages rose and locked into the ceiling.

"Who are you?" Kiya yelled as she crouched.

"You don't know do you? I am disappointed. I thought your people would have told stories about me." Kiya looked at him oddly. "Do you remember Shayla?" he asked.

Kiya tried to remember. Then, it hit her. *'Oh yes, Shayla. The little girl that was stolen from my village when I was just a mere child myself.'* Kiya wasn't afraid of many things but this she was afraid of. "You're The Collector!" Kiya said.

"Very good," he said as he grabbed a staff that was nicely hidden next to the control panel.

"Sorry Kiya," Tabitha said. "I should have listened to you."

Kiya focused her attention on The Collector. "Why did you take Shayla?" Kiya asked indignantly.

"I collect people," he responded. "It is what I do. I had to have a mighty Dambroo warrior."

"But she was just a child," Kiya protested.

"Yes, easier to capture," he said.

"What have you done with her?" Kiya asked. "Where is she?"

"I'm afraid she became ill and passed on. But you could take her place," he said with a grin as he approached her. "I appreciate your contribution of these two nice American subjects but with Shayla's passing I have no Dambroo. So, I'm going to have to ask you to stay."

"I don't think so!" she said as she jumped and kicked The Collector in the chest. He stumbled back and swung his staff at her legs, tripping her. She fell to the ground and returned the favor, tripping him with her legs. They both got up and Kiya kicked The Collector in the head. He stumbled backwards and fell to the ground next to the control panel. Kiya went over to the control panel and looked for the button with the symbols that matched the square he was on. She found them and pushed the button. A cage quickly rose from the gaps and trapped The Collector.

"Very good," he said. "But not good enough." The Collector reached his hands through the bars and pushed two buttons on the control panel. They were different then the other buttons. These had no symbols on them. Suddenly, bars crossed the doors and locked them shut. There was a countdown on the control panel.

"What is that?" Kiya asked.

"I activated the self destruct mechanism," he said. "That is how long before the ship explodes."

Tabitha looked over to Michelle inside their cages. "Oh no," she said.

"What?" Michelle asked. "What is going on?"

"The whole ship is going to explode," Tabby answered.

"How do I shut it off?" Kiya yelled to The Collector.

"You must enter the code," he said.

"What is it?" she asked eagerly.

"My name, Arnemore."

"I don't know your lettering," she panicked.

"But I do," he said with an evil grin.

"Tell me what to push!" she yelled as she punched him through the bars of the cage. He stumbled back against the other side of the cage. "Tell me or I'll kill you," she yelled.

"Silly child," he said. "If you kill me we all die. Let me out and you can live."

"Fine, how do I let you out?" she asked.

"You push the same button that locked me in," he said.

Kiya picked up his staff and looked over to Michelle and Tabby. She pushed the buttons on the control panel that matched their squares. Their cages began to lower. Then she reluctantly released Arnemore. "Now shut it off!" Kiya yelled. Arnemore went to the control panel and pushed a series of buttons that stopped the timer. "Now open the door," Kiya added as she held the staff to his throat.

The gray skin around his mouth rippled with a smile. "You don't want me to take the Americans home?" he asked.

"Not to your home!" Tabitha said.

"You don't trust me?" he asked.

"No," Kiya said. "Now let us go."

He hit a couple of buttons. The bars across the doors released and retracted into the ship. The door opened to reveal the sandy desert.

"Now be gone," The Collector said. "But hear this; I will be back for my Dambroo warrior. And if you Americans are still here, you are fair game also."

"And you'll get your ass kicked again," Tabitha responded in English. They exited the ship with their backs to the smiling Arnemore. The door closed as the girls walked toward the forest.

Tom and the others were just entering the desert as the ship lifted off.

"No!" Jade yelled as she ran to the ship with a tear in her eyes. Tabitha stopped her with a hug. "There goes our ride home," Jade said.

"You don't want that ride," Tabby said.

"What happened?" Tom asked.

The girls explained as they all started back to their ship.

8

William and Sara had finished with all the packing.

"So why are you suddenly not interested in me?" William asked.

"I just think that Jade is more your type," Sara responded.

"I don't know," William said. "Jade is complicated and you're..."

"Easy?" Sara interjected. The slight anger on her face was apparent. William thought carefully of his response to this so he didn't cause an argument. He could not come up with anything clever though.

"Well, no. I was going to say not complicated," he answered.

"Well I'm not easy," Sara said.

"Okay, I never said that you were. It's just that when I'm with you I understand what you're feeling and what you want. With Jade I have no clue. She doesn't open up. I'm still not even sure if she likes me."

"She likes you," Sara said bluntly.

"I know she likes me, but how much?" he asked.

"Why don't you ask her that?" Sara suggested. "If you sat her down and talked to her alone, she would open up to you."

"You're right. Thanks," he said as he hugged her.

9

The others were making their way back home when Michelle pulled Kiya aside. "Thank you for saving our lives," she said.

"You would have done the same," Kiya answered.

"No, I would have tried but probably failed. If it weren't for you we would all probably be dead. I'm just trying to say that we appreciate you staying with us. It can't be easy being away from your village."

"Well, I had to get away for awhile. My people take me for granted. They don't mean to but they do. I do lot of hunting and protect them a great deal. They need to learn to survive without me. I won't be around forever."

"What do you mean?" Michelle asked. "Your only in your twenties."

"Did you look around my village?" Kiya asked. "How many old people did you see? We have no one as old as Tom. Most of our people are lucky if they live as long as I have. We don't live that long out here."

Michelle had never really paid attention before. Kiya was right. Queen Laza and Jango were about the oldest people she remembered.

They reached the field and headed toward the ship. *'This was the first test of Sara's friendship,'* Jade thought. Sara and William approached them.

"So are we going home?" William asked.

"I'm afraid not," Simonson answered. They explained what had happened to Sara and William. After cooking and eating the Gallimimus egg, everyone went inside and settled down for bed as the two suns had gone down.

10

William decided that it was time for his talk with Jade. He asked her to meet him outside by the fire. He sat down and stared at the flames as he waited. The fire seemed to be alive. He watched it jumping and leaping. The flames were fluttering around. Then, he turned his attention toward the sky. He thought of how he would word this. His wording was important. He thought as he watched the stars sparkling throughout the sky. Jade came out and sat next to him with a smile.

"Jade," he said as he grabbed her hand. "I like you... a lot."

"That's fine," Jade answered. "But I'm not going to get all giggly when I'm around you. I'm just not that way."

"I don't care. I just don't want you to be so defensive about everything. Don't you get it? I like you. I want to be with you."

"Fine, I'll try not to be so defensive. I don't know about us though William."

"What? Why not?" he asked.

"I'm not sure we should see each other."

"Why not?" he asked.

"I don't know," Jade answered. "I just don't want the others to… I don't know. I just don't think it's a good idea."

"Why not? We don't have to be all lovey dovey. I just want to be able to spend some quality alone time with you."

"Alright," she agreed. "Hey, I'm just curious; did Sara try flirting with you today?"

"Actually no. She didn't," he answered.

"Good," Jade said. "You better not hurt me William."

"I won't hurt you," he said as he leaned over and kissed her. They went inside and went to their separate beds and called it a night.

Chapter Thirteen:
The Journey North

1

It was another bright and sunny morning on the planet. Coy, O'Dell, Simonson, and Paul were gathered by the fire pit. Sara and Michelle had already left for a water run. The others were all inside but the ship door was open.

"We should explore farther," O'Dell said. "Maybe there is someone with a ship or some fuel."

"I don't know," Tom said. "It may be too dangerous to keep exploring."

"Besides, this planet is far less advanced than Earth," Paul added.

"I wouldn't say less advanced," Simonson mentioned. "This planet has just advanced differently. Earth may have the technology that this planet doesn't, but the predators here have developed extraordinary hunting skills. That is why I'm not sure it's a good idea to go exploring."

"Kiya has managed to stay alive out here for over twenty years. It might be more dangerous to not go looking for a way home. I'm not sure we all would last as long as Kiya," O'Dell stated.

Kiya and Tabby walked outside and joined them.

"What are you guys talking about?" Tabitha asked.

"We are trying to decide if it is a good idea to go explore farther."

"Explore in which direction?" Kiya asked.

"I don't know…north I guess," Michael said. "Past the plains."

"The Pondera Patoona is past the plains," Kiya said.

"Great," Simonson said. "What is the Pondera Patoona?"

"Well, Pondera is a type of insect I guess, and Patoona in your language would be… tunnels," Kiya explained.

"So there's insect tunnels," Coy said. "Big deal."

"I still want to go," O'Dell said plainly.

"If you insist," Simonson said. "Let's get the tents and see who all wants to go."

"I'll go," Tabitha said cheerfully.

"Kiya?" Michael asked.

"Yeah, someone has to look out for you Americans," she joked. Tom entered the ship to ask the others.

Jade walked over to William who was sleeping. She bent down and woke him with a peck on the lips.

"Good morning," he said with a smile.

"I overheard the others talking about going north today," she said. "Do you want to go?"

"If we stayed here it would give us a chance to spend some quality time together," he said.

"I didn't ask you if we wanted to go, I asked you if you wanted to go. I'm going," she said sternly.

"Well then. I guess I'm going too," he answered.

Tom entered as William finished. "So you are both going, great," he said as he left.

Tom rejoined the others at the fire pit.

"So who's going?" Coy asked.

"Everyone so far. I'll ask Sara and Michelle when they return with the water," Simonson said. When they returned an hour later he asked them and they also decided to go.

2

Everyone gathered the needed supplies and began their journey north. Michael and Wesley scouted ahead to the cannibal camp. They crouched behind a bush and peered through. There were about fifteen cannibals sitting around the fire. They quietly went back to the others without being spotted.

"We have to go around the camp," Wesley said.

"Make sure we stay quiet until we are far away," O'Dell added.

Tom suddenly noticed that Michael was carrying a spear instead of the gun. "Where's the gun," Simonson asked.

"I left it back at camp."

"What?" Tom yelled.

"Shhh!" O'Dell said as he pointed back toward the cannibal camp.

Tom waited until they were clear from the cannibal camp. "How did you forget the gun?" he asked irritated.

"I didn't forget it," Michael said. "I left it behind on purpose."

"Why on Earth would you do that?" Tom yelled.

William smiled, "We're not on Earth, Tom."

"Honey no," Jade said as she grabbed his arm.

Tom shot angry look at William and returned his focus on Michael.

"We don't need the gun," Michael said. "We are relying on it too much. Plus, we have to conserve ammo."

"This is totally irresponsible," Professor Simonson barked. "You know as well as I that we have plenty of ammo. You've just put all of our lives in danger!"

"Our lives are in danger every day out here!" O'Dell snapped back. "We need to learn to take care of ourselves without the gun. We won't have ammo forever."

"We have plenty of ammo," Tom responded. "How long do you expect to be on this planet?"

"Well I didn't even expect to be out here this long," O'Dell answered. "We have to prepare for the worst case scenario. We may be here forever. That is why I left it behind."

"Okay," Michelle interjected. "What's done is done. We don't need to argue. Let's just deal with it."

"You're right," Tom agreed.

3

The explorers had reached the Great Plains. There were plant-eating dinosaurs everywhere. The grass was green and the collage of wildlife was breathtaking. There were several Triceratops, Stegosaurus, Ankylosaurus, and other tank-like herbivores. There were also Gallimimus and Struthiomimus grazing near each other. They were small compared to another two-legged giant that was standing near.

"What is that?' Coy asked Michelle.

"Iguanadon," Michelle answered. It stood nearly as tall as a T-Rex would. There were also Brontosaurus and Brachiosaurus present. The gentle giants looked even more magnificent in the open plains. Everyone stood there and took in the view.

"This is beautiful," Michelle said.

"In deed it is," Professor Simonson agreed.

They began to walk into the open across the Great Plains. Most of the dinosaurs ignored them and continued their feast. Some of the Struthiomimus popped their heads up and began to run. They quickly stopped when they noticed the humans were uninterested and didn't give chase.

4

Kiya walked over next to Coy. "So do you have a family?" she asked him.

"No, I haven't found the right girl yet."

"What about your mother," she asked.

"Yuk! Kiya, in our culture you don't do that stuff with your mother. Besides, I don't really have a mother."

"That is what I meant silly," she said as she giggled. "I meant what happened to your mother?"

"Well, I never really had one," Coy answered.

Kiya looked puzzled. "You were born, you must have had a mother," she insisted.

"The lady who gave birth to me put me up for adoption," Coy responded.

Kiya still looked puzzled. "What is adoption?" she asked.

"She didn't want me so she gave me away. I went to two different families when I was young, but they both brought me back to the orphanage. I lived there until I was eighteen. Then I got an apartment of my own."

"What is this orphanage?" Kiya asked.

"An orphanage is where unwanted children grow up. The orphanage tries to find families that want the children. Sometimes when the kids get too old they end up living at the orphanage because nobody wants them. I stayed there because nobody wanted me."

Kiya smiled up at Coy and put her arm up around his shoulder. "We want you Coy," she said. "We are your family now."

"Gee thanks Kiya," Coy said as he smiled down at her.

5

William and Jade were taking in the breathtaking view. "Isn't this beautiful?" he asked.

"Yeah," she agreed. "Let's just hope they all stay friendly."

"They're all plant eaters," William mentioned. "What are you worried about?"

"I just don't trust creatures that are that huge. One swing of a tail or wrong step and we could be done. I just don't want to get too close."

"Don't worry about it. We'll be fine," he said as he draped his arm around her shoulder.

Sara was in deep thought. She wished her father were here right now. She felt a sense of peace come over her.

"What ya thinking about?" Wesley asked.

"Nothing. I'm just glad you're all here." Sara said to everyone. "I mean it. If we get home, you guys will all have a million dollars but I'll have all of you as my friends. I haven't been exactly nice to everyone but I want you all to know that I do care."

"We are kind of like family now," Tabby added. Everyone smiled in one of the few peaceful moments they have had on this planet.

6

They all continued walking through the Great Plains all day. They came to a forest with only about two hours of daylight left. Michael suggested that they make camp in the plains and continue in the morning. Everyone agreed and they set up the tents. Michael, Tom, and Paul went in one tent and went to bed. The others gathered in the other tent and formed a circle and chatted for a while.

"So, I see you two are an item now," Tabitha said to William and Jade.

"Yeah, I guess you could say that," Jade responded.

"What about you Coy?" Michelle asked. "Have you ever been in a serious relationship?"

"Uh, no. Most girls just pick on me," he answered. "Once I had a crush on a girl named Angie when I was in school. Her friend called me and told me that Angie liked me. So, I called her and asked her out."

"So what happened?" Tabby asked.

"She laughed at me and said 'no way.' I realized then that her friend had told me as a joke."

"That's awful," Michelle said. "You must have been devastated."

"No, I guess not. At least I knew what she was like and no longer had a crush on her."

"I think that is a good way to look at it," Sara said.

"What about you Kiya?" William asked. "Did you ever have a long relationship?"

"No," she answered. "The man who was supposed to be my partner died when I was about twelve."

"Twelve? How old was he?" Sara asked.

"He was about three years older. We have arranged partnerships. I am still pure."

"Pure? You mean a virgin?" William asked.

"I have never had sex," Kiya commented.

"Holy cow!" William said as he smiled. His smile faded when he saw that Jade was not amused with his interest in Kiya's sexual history.

"What about you Michelle?" Sara asked.

"What, virgin?" Michelle said as she laughed.

"No, I mean have you ever been in a serious relationship," Sara reiterated.

"No, Tabby and I used to party a lot in college."

"Oh yeah?" William asked. "You ever kiss a girl?"

Michelle smiled and looked over to Tabby who had an equally big grin on her face. "Yeah, I've messed around with a girl before," Michelle answered.

William's eyes grew big like those of a child's on Christmas morning right before opening his presents. "Continue," he said.

"I'm going to bed," Jade commented as she got up and switched tents.

"William, you just pissed her off," Sara stated.

"So, we're not married. She'll get over it," he replied. "Go ahead, continue," he said to Michelle who was smiling and shaking her head.

"Why don't we just show him what we used to do," Tabby suggested. William's eyes grew large with anticipation. Coy and Wesley's attention were also focused on Tabby who was sliding over next to Michelle.

Michelle put her hand on Tabitha's face and gently kissed her on the lips. "I don't remember the rest," she quickly joked.

"Yeah, we were pretty drunk," Tabby added.

"You guys were just pulling my leg weren't you," William yelled as Sara laughed.

"No, we did mess around," Michelle said with a smile. "But you're not privileged enough to see what we did."

"Forget it," William said as he angrily got up and walked out. This sent Sara and Wesley into uncontrollable laughter. Even Coy was chuckling.

"We better turn in," Michelle said. "It is getting late."

They all agreed as they went to sleep.

7

William entered the other tent to see Jade and the others fast asleep. He quietly lay down next to her. He put his arm around her but she quickly batted it off.

"Go cuddle with your lesbo friends," Jade said hastily.

"They were only joking," William said.

"I could care less what they have done," Jade replied. "But I don't need to see you slobbering all over them."

"I wasn't," he pleaded.

"It's late and I want to get to bed," Jade said. "I don't care about tonight okay. But if you so much as kiss another girl, you're done. You don't get a second chance with me. Do you understand?"

"Yeah," he said as they went to bed. Both tents were now silent as everyone slept through the peaceful night.

8

Michael was the first to wake as usual. He looked outside to see the Great Plains were empty of dinosaurs except a small herd of Gallimimus that stood on the edge by the forest. Suddenly the Gallimimus started running toward him and the others. *'What's going on,'* he wondered. Then a T-Rex emerged from the forest. The Gallimimus were not running toward him but away from the T-Rex. Unfortunately their escape route was in the direction of the tents. "Wake up!" O'Dell yelled.

Kiya had poked her head out of the other tent. "Stay inside and stay quiet," she yelled over to O'Dell. He nodded and went back in his tent. Kiya also returned to her tent.

"Kiya, stay inside?" Sara said with doubt. "They are leading the T-Rex right this way."

"I know, look around. We're in the middle of a field. Do you think you can outrun it? Our only chance is to stay inside." They all sat there and watched through the windows of their tents. William was holding Jade in his arms as he watched with Michael. The Gallimimus ran past the tents. Some were inches from them. The ground was shaking from the T-Rex who was still in pursuit. A few seconds after the Gallimimus was the T-Rex who continued on after the Gallimimus.

"Okay, lets go," Sara said as she got up.

Kiya tackled her. "We can't go out there," she said.

"Why? He passed us. He is chasing the Gallimimus."

"He won't catch the Gallimimus," Kiya said. "He will give up soon."

They watched as the T-Rex stopped its chase.

"I hate it that you are always right," Sara said.

"I am no better than you," Kiya explained. "I just know my home and its creatures better."

They all waited as the T-Rex walked off into the distance. "Okay, we should be safe now," Kiya said. She exited the tent. "Let's leave before he comes back," she said as everyone exited and quickly dismantled the tents.

9

They continued walking north and entered the forest. It was mainly pines and ferns. The needles were scattered across the forest's floor. Tabitha took a great interest in all the ferns. She was stopping and looking at the different varieties.

"This is beautiful," she said as she looked at a unique fern in her hand. It was only about four feet tall but had very large green and purple leaves.

"It's a plant," Sara said bluntly.

"Plants are my life," Tabitha responded.

"I guess whatever turns you on," Sara said as she turned back around.

William and Jade were bring up the rear and chatting to each other.

"Did you enjoy last night," Jade asked.

"Yeah, up until our disagreement," he answered.

"Well, I'm sorry. I just felt like I was third on your attention list."

"I'm sorry too," he said.

"It's okay," Jade said with a sincere smile. "Any normal guy would get turned on by two hot chicks messing around."

"Oh so you think they're hot?" he asked.

"Don't get any ideas. I'm not doing anything with a girl," Jade said with a smile.

William kissed her and they caught up with the others.

Chapter Fourteen:
Pondera Patoona

1

After about two hours of walking the forest gave way to a small desert. They began walking across the sand until Kiya stopped them. Everyone had spaced themselves out now that they weren't in the thick forest. "Careful," she said. "The Pondera set traps."

"What do you mean set traps?" Michael asked. "They're insects." He found out on his next step as he, Tom, and Paul fell through the sand and disappeared.

"Tom!" Michelle yelled as she ran across the desert toward where the fell through.

"No," William yelled as he ran after her and tackled her to the ground, which also gave way.

"Be careful everyone," Kiya said as she turned to see that Sara, Jade, and Tabby had also disappeared. Suddenly the ground gave way as Kiya, Coy and Wesley fell into the darkness.

2

As Michael stood up he shook the dirt off. He went over and helped Tom and Paul to their feet. They were in a large tunnel. The only light was coming from the hole above them. It was about fifteen feet up. "Well, left or right?" O'Dell asked.

"I don't care," Tom said. "You have the spear, lead the way."

Meanwhile William and Michelle were getting up from the ground as well. She tossed him her spear. "Oh, I'm supposed to protect you?" he asked.

"Sure, give it a shot." she answered.

"This isn't cool that we all got separated," he commented.

"Yeah, but at least we aren't alone. Let's go look for Tom, Paul, and Michael." As they walked deeper into the tunnel the light faded into complete darkness. "Uh, maybe we should hold hands," she suggested.

"Okay," he answered as he reached for her with his free hand. It brushed against her stomach. He could feel her slight indented bellybutton through her shirt. She reached down and grabbed his hand as they continued to walk.

3

Coy, Kiya, and Wesley were walking in the darkness with a different system. Kiya led the way. Coy followed with a hand on her shoulder. Wesley followed them with a hand on Coy's shoulder.

"What lives in here?" Coy asked.

"Pondera," Kiya answered.

"That insect you talked about?" Wesley asked.

"Yes."

"But why would an insect live in a tunnel that is fifteen feet high?" Wesley asked.

"The Pondera is rather large, and it isn't one but many."

"Oh shit," Wesley said. "Why does it always have to be a Raptor or a giant scorpion or a T-Rex? Why can't it ever be a tribe of women that are craving sex? Can't we ever get a break? Insects are supposed to be small!"

"I'm guessing these Pondera are pretty dangerous?" Coy asked.

"Yes," Kiya replied as they walked through the darkness.

4

Jade had her spear out as Tabby, Sara and her began to walk into the darkness.

"We should hold hands," Sara suggested.

"I'm not holding hands with you two!" Jade objected. Jade continued to walk in front as Sara and Tabby held hands behind her. Before long it became completely dark. They stayed silent as they walked through the darkness. Sara reached her hand out for Jade and brushed against her butt.

"Hey!" Jade snapped. "What the hell are you doing?"

"Well I don't want to lose you," Sara replied.

"Well I don't want to get felt up either!"

"That is why we should hold hands," Sara suggested.

"Great, I have to decide whether to hold your hand or get molested by you. Fine!"

Jade reached back for Sara and her hand touched Sara's breast. "Ooh, Jade," Sara joked.

"Knock it off bitch. Just give me your damn hand!" They held hands and continued.

5

O'Dell, Finch, and Simonson were verbally checking to see if they were close. Every couple seconds O'Dell would do a roll call to make sure they were still close. Up ahead about thirty feet was a glowing green light. It illuminated the tunnel enough to see a corner ahead. The light was coming from around the corner. "Look," Tom said. "Something's coming." O'Dell raised the spear and prepared for the worst. The green light became brighter as it emerged from around the corner.

"What the hell is that?" O'Dell asked.

"I'm guessing that it's the insect Kiya called Pondera," Tom answered. The creature was about four feet tall with a single antenna that protruded from its head. The green light was coming from the top of the antenna. "It's luminescent," Tom commented.

"Excuse me?" O'Dell said.

"It provides its own light," Tom explained, "similar to a lightning bug or some deep see fishes."

The Pondera slowly advanced toward them. It was now about fifteen feet away from them. It had one solid body similar to a spider. The Pondera walked on four spiny legs and had two large black eyes that glowed green from the shine of its light. Its mouth hosted two large fangs and one sharp stinger in between them. As it approached, Michael prepared to spear it. The Pondera made a hissing sound and its stinger shot forward like a spear. O'Dell dove and knocked Tom down with him. The stinger impaled Paul in the chest. It pulled him toward the Pondera as Michael threw his spear. The spear stuck in the Pondera's head as it let out a shriek.

6

The shriek echoed through the tunnels. "What was that?" Sara asked in fear.

"I don't want to know," Tabby answered. Jade raised her spear but in the darkness it was impossible to see anything. They slowly continued with their hands clutched tightly together. They noticed a green light up ahead. It came closer and closer until they noticed the Pondera crawling on the ceiling toward them.

"What is that?" Sara asked frightened.

"What do we do?" Tabby asked. "Do we run back the way we came?"

"No! We kill the fucking thing!" Jade yelled as she released Sara's hand and charged forward. She threw the spear up at the creature and connected perfectly in its abdomen. The Pondera screeched and dropped to the floor, impaling itself more when the ground pushed the spear almost through it.

"Good shot girl," Tabby said. Sara ran over to Jade and hugged her.

"Will you get off me? It's bad enough I have to hold your hand."

"Sorry," Sara said with a smile. Jade pulled the spear out of the dead Pondera and they continued on.

7

Tom and O'Dell approached the dead Pondera and their fallen friend. Both were lifeless on the floor of the tunnel. "I'm sorry," O'Dell said.

"It's not your fault," Tom replied.

"If I had brought the gun, maybe we could have shot it?"

"No," Tom said. "None of us knew the stinger would eject like that. You would have had the same reaction to dive out of the way. Nothing would have changed. Don't beat yourself up, we need you to protect the rest of us."

"I'll do my best," O'Dell said.

"Help me pull him off the stinger," Tom said as he grabbed Paul's arm. Michael did the same and they yanked his body off the stinger and lowered him to the ground. "He was a good man," Tom said. Michael nodded.

Tom walked over to the Pondera and began inspecting it. "This creature is fascinating. Do you have your knife?"

"This is hardly the time to dissect it Professor."

"Oh I don't want to dissect it. I want to borrow its light."

"Good idea," Michael said as he pulled the knife out began cutting the Pondera's antenna off.

"Now we will be able to see," Tom said as he held up the glowing, severed antenna.

8

William and Michelle were still hand in hand walking through the darkness. There was a sound coming from ahead. They squeezed each other's hands in anticipation.

"What's that," Michelle whispered.

"Stand behind me," William responded. He raised the spear and they waited as they heard the sound getting closer. As soon as the sound was directly in front of him he thrust his spear forward. Something grabbed the spear and took it away from him. Then he was tripped by his own spear.

"Nice welcome," a female voice said.

"Kiya?" William asked as he stood up.

"Yeah. Who did you think it was?"

"Is anyone with you," Michelle asked.

"Coy and I are with her," Wesley stated. "Any sign of the others?"

"No," Michelle answered. "We haven't seen anything."

Suddenly there was a green light coming from the direction Kiya, Coy, and Wesley came.

"What the hell is that? William asked.

"Pondera," Kiya answered. "Stay back," she said as she held her spear up. Sand sprinkled down onto Wesley's face.

"Get back! We're under a trap," he yelled. They backed up away from the Pondera and the trap in the ceiling. Suddenly the light poured in as a Raptor fell down from above right between the explorers and the Pondera.

"Oh shit," William said as fear came over them. There was no outrunning a Raptor in these dark small tunnels.

"Great," Michelle said as she slowly backed away. "As if the giant insect wasn't enough. Now we have to deal with a Raptor too!" The Raptor stumbled to its feet. It crouched and pounced toward Michelle. It was stopped in midair by the impaling stinger from the Pondera behind it. The Raptor body was pulled toward the Pondera as the insect began to feast.

"Come on let's go!" Kiya said as they quickly walked away.

9

Sara, Tabby, and Jade continued to walk through the darkness as a green light approached from the front.

"Great, we've got company ahead," Tabby said.

"They're slow, I'll kill it," Jade said confidently. They walked forward with Jade leading the way. When they got close they saw that it wasn't a Pondera after all. "Relax," Jade said. "It's just Tom and Michael."

"That's sick!" Sara said as she pointed to the severed antenna.

"Hey at least we can see," O'Dell said.

"Where's Paul?" Tabitha asked.

"I'm afraid he didn't make it," Michael said.

Tabitha put her hands up to her face. She wiped a tear as the sorrow set in. They had lost another friend. First Steve Hanson and now Paul Finch.

"There is nothing we can do about that now," O'Dell said. "We have to make sure the rest of us get out of here alright."

"Any sign of the others?" Tom asked.

"No," Tabby replied. "You?"

"Well we heard some noise coming from one of the sub-tunnels back there," Tom said.

"It sounded like a Raptor," Michael added.

"Well I sure as hell don't want to meet a Raptor down here," Sara said.

"We should check that way for the others though," Tom said. "I thought I might have heard Michelle but I'm not certain."

"Why didn't you guys go that way already?" Sara asked.

"We're not crazy about meeting a Raptor down here either," Tom said. "Plus I was unsure if I heard Michelle's voice, but could definitely hear the racket you guys made."

"Sorry," Tabby said with a grin.

"That's why we came to get you guys first," O'Dell added. "This way if there is a Raptor we have two spears instead of one."

"Alright, let's go," Jade said impatiently. "If you heard Michelle, William should be with her. They fell through together."

"Let's hope so," Tom said. "I wouldn't want to be down here by myself."

Suddenly a green light appeared ahead. "No time to talk. We've got a bug to kill," O'Dell said as he raised his spear. Jade joined him in front of the others who stood by the wall of the tunnel. Jade threw her spear and hit the Pondera's leg but it continued toward them. It shot its stinger out and Jade dove to avoid being hit. O'Dell drove his spear down through the Pondera as it let out a shriek.

10

Meanwhile, William and the others were walking toward a bright green glow. They approached a large opening in the tunnels. They were standing at the edge of their tunnel looking down into a large chamber. The drop must have been fifty feet. There were green lights everywhere.

"There must be a hundred Pondera down there," Kiya said. "We have to go back the other way."

"Let's rest a while," Coy said. Everyone agreed as they sat down by the edge of the chamber.

11

"This is just my luck," William said. "I've had bad luck my whole life."

"You haven't had bad luck," Michelle said. "It's just how you look at things. The glass is half full William."

"Yeah okay," he disagreed. "When I was twelve my parents hired a clown for my birthday party."

"Well that was nice," Michelle said.

"No it wasn't. He was supposed to do magic. He ended up massacring a rabbit in front of everyone and my parents refused to pay him."

"Okay, that's bad, but it's not horrible. It wasn't your rabbit was it?" she asked.

"No, but the clown got mad and ran off with all my birthday cards and money."

"Okay, but that doesn't mean you have bad luck. That was just one bad incident."

"Okay, how about this one; When I was seventeen, I had a girlfriend whose mom wasn't fond of me. One night my friend Shawn and I were driving around and decided to stop at a gas station and get some things. He got some Junior Mints and I got some Skittles and a soda. I put the Skittles on the dash and the soda in my cup holder. When we drove off Shawn mentioned that he forgot to get a soda. It was no big deal because Chelsea lived on the block that the gas station was located on and I wanted to go by her house anyway. As we approached the intersection facing her house, my Skittles popped open and started rolling across the dash. I reached up to stop them and my elbow hit the headlights and they flickered. This startled me and my knee knocked over my soda. My right hand was busy with the Skittles so I reached down to pick it up with my left but my shoulder hit the horn. After getting everything settled, we returned to the gas station and Shawn got a soda. As we pulled away to go home a cop pulled us over. This was odd. I knew I was doing the speed limit. He came to the window and asked me to get out of the car. A police officer never asks you to get out of the car unless it's serious. I followed him to the back of the car and he asked me if I knew why he had pulled me over. I didn't have a clue so I told him no.

The policeman became very irritated. 'You know damn well why I pulled you over,' he yelled. 'You've been harassing your girlfriend's mom; honking your horn and flashing your lights!' I wasn't about to tell him what really happened. There is no way he would believe it was a coincidence."

Michelle was laughing hysterically at this point. "Okay," she said. "I guess you do have bad luck."

12

O'Dell and the others came across the half-eaten Raptor carcass. "I guess that ruckus was a Raptor," O'Dell commented.

"That's fucking pleasant," Sara said as she glanced at the mutilated carcass.

"Let's just hope that the others got away," Tom said. They continued on. Sara looked over to see a tear rolling down Jade's cheek.

"What's wrong, Jade?" she whispered.

"Nothing, " Jade quickly replied.

Sara could see that Jade was concerned about William. "Don't worry," Sara said. "He'll be alright." She put her arm around Jade.

"You don't know that," Jade said as she wiped the tear off her cheek.

"Well, no… wait," Sara said as she looked ahead. "Actually I do know. He's sitting up there by that bright green glow."

Jade looked and could see William, Michelle, Coy, Wesley, and Kiya all sitting by the edge of the large opening.

"William!" Jade yelled with joy as she ran toward him.

"Oh shit," William said as he looked in the chamber to see that Jade's yell had alerted the Pondera. Several of them had started up the wall toward them.

"Come on!" William said as he grabbed Michelle's hand. William, Michelle, and the others joined the rest of the explorers as the Pondera continued their slow steady pursuit.

"We have to get out of here," Tabitha said.

"Yeah, but how?" William asked.

"I think I have an idea," O'Dell said. "Follow me." He led them to the Raptor carcass.

"What's your idea?" Sara asked.

"We're going out this hole," he said as he pointed up.

"How?" Sara asked. "It's like twenty feet up and we have no rope."

"Get your spears ready," O'Dell said. Michael, William, Kiya, and Jade stepped forward with spears in hand.

"We're going to fight all of them?" William asked.

"Yes, we are going to kill the bastards. Just watch out for their stingers."

"You're crazy!" William said.

"Do you have a better idea?" O'Dell asked.

"Yeah, run."

"Running won't get us out of here," Michael said.

13

Some of the Pondera were approaching now. They had distanced themselves from the main pack. Michael speared one as it closed in. Jade killed the next one. Kiya and William killed the next two. They kept killing the persistent Pondera. The bodies were piling up but the next wave of Pondera simply climbed over.

"Kill them while they're on top of the dead ones," O'Dell said. A pile started to form. O'Dell and the others climbed up to battle the charging Pondera. There must have been twenty dead already and the tunnel was starting to fill up with bodies. One of the Pondera launched its stinger at William. He stepped aside and dodged it but lost his footing. He fell off the pile and landed about ten feet down on the tunnel's floor. Michelle ran over and grabbed his spear. She killed the Pondera as Tabby and Coy helped William up. Michelle made her way to the top of the pile and took William's place. The pile of Pondera bodies grew larger and larger until the tunnel was sealed. There was a wall of bodies dividing the explorers and the Pondera.

"Climb up," O'Dell yelled down to the others.

"You want us to climb up these dead, bloody insects?" Sara asked.

"Well, only if you want to get out," he said as he pulled himself out of the tunnel. The sunlight was blinding but was a relief. Kiya, Michelle, and Jade pulled themselves out as well. Tabby and Tom began to climb the pile. They hurried as the sound of the frantic Pondera on the other side grew. Coy, Wesley, and William climbed up next. Sara was now alone at the bottom of the pile.

"Come on Sara," William yelled. She reluctantly began climbing the pile. Suddenly, a stinger shot through the pile from the other side. It narrowly missed her head. "Hurry!" William yelled as he lay down on the sand with his arm outstretched. She grabbed it and he pulled her up. Another stinger shot through just missing her feet as she was raised to the sand. They both stood up and brushed off.

14

Everyone walked toward home except William, Jade, and Sara.

"Thank you!" Sara said as she hugged him and planted a kiss on his cheek. Jade looked on with peeked interest. Sara knew she'd be upset but didn't care. That moment was between her and William. She felt safe in his arms. *'Jade doesn't deserve someone as great as William,'* she thought.

"Yeah, you're welcome," Jade said. "Now get off him."

"I was just relieved to be alive," Sara explained as she smiled.

"Yeah, sure," Jade replied. "You're still the same old Sara. I don't trust you one bit. Our deal is off."

"Fine," Sara grinned. "But surely you trust him, right?" Sara knew that this was going to plant a wedge between Jade and William. She could get William to doubt Jade's trust in him.

"Just keep your paws off him," Jade insisted.

Sara backed away with her hands up. "You didn't answer the question, Jade." They all started walking toward the others but stayed at a safe talking distance.

"I don't need to answer any question coming from you."

"Well, I'd still like to know," William said. "Do you trust me?"

'God damn it,' Jade thought. *'That bitch knew exactly what she was doing all along.'*

"Well?" William asked.

"What?" Jade snapped.

"Do you trust me?"

"William honey, can't you see? Sara is just trying to get us to argue."

"You don't trust me do you?" he asked angrily. Sara was all smiles as Jade squirmed.

"I trust the fact that you care about me and you don't want to hurt me, but I don't think you can say no to someone who's seducing you."

"Bullshit!" he yelled. "I have a mind of my own. I can control myself."

"Let's test that theory," Sara said with a smile.

"You stay the fuck out of it!" Jade yelled. "In fact, stay away from him completely."

"Why? You don't think he can control himself around me?" Sara asked. "Or are you worried that he might enjoy spending time with me more than you."

"That's it bitch!" Jade snapped as she stepped toward Sara with her fists clenched.

William grabbed Jade and held her back. "And you think I need control," he said.

"Well William, you can see that she's a fighter and I'm a lover. Any time you want a lover you come and see me sweetie," Sara said as she turned and caught up with the others.

"Let go of me!" Jade said as she shook herself free of his grasp.

"You can't fight your way out of everything, Jade."

"Yeah, well that snotty, rich, whore needs her ass kicked and I'd be glad to do it."

"I think you need to be more understanding," William said.

"Are you fucking crazy? She was all over you! If you want to mess around that's fine, but I'm not going to be a part of it. If you want her, go get her. If you want to be with me, you need to stay away from her."

"Sara and I are just friends," William said. "That's all we'll ever be. You need to deal with it because I'm not going to be mean to her just because you don't like her."

"Whatever," Jade replied.

15

The others were still far ahead of William and Jade. They were walking at a good pace but Sara caught up.

"Why do you have to get them arguing?" Tabby asked her.

"It makes things more interesting," Sara replied.

"Well things are interesting enough out here with Pondera, Apemen, Cannibals, and Raptors. We don't need your help to make things interesting."

"Well aren't we a little bitchy today?" Sara responded.

"Out here we need to be able to trust each other. Excuse me if I question your intentions when you cause suspense."

"Tabitha's right," O'Dell added. "You're damaging the mission."

Sara became furious. "I don't need your lectures. Who's damaging the mission when you didn't even bring the fucking gun! Keep in mind who is responsible for this mission."

"Sara," Tom said. "We all know that this mission would not have happened without you. But don't you want to be responsible for a successful mission not a failure? It's a failure if we all die."

Sara just snarled and looked away.

"We should stop and make camp," Tom said. He and O'Dell set up one tent while Michelle and Tabby set the other up. Kiya and Coy were watching and Sara and Wesley sat off to the side. William and Jade were still catching up.

"Sara," Wesley said. "You can't expect these people to understand you. You are rich and have always gotten your way. You are everything that society hates."

"What about you?" Sara asked. "Do you hate me?"

"Of course not. I'd do you in a second," he smiled.

"Pig," Sara laughed.

"I'm just saying that you should lighten up on Jade. She doesn't like you and she is tough as hell. Do you really want to piss her off?"

"Oh I do Wes," Sara said with a smile. "I enjoy it more than you know. I don't care if she kicks the shit out of me as long as I get one good shot in."

"You're crazy," he said.

16

William and Jade had caught up now and the tents were set. The sky was getting dark and the plain's only inhabitants were some Gallimimus. O'Dell, Simonson, Coy, Kiya, and Wesley all went to bed in one tent. Tabby,

Michelle, William, and Jade were all lying down in the other tent when Sara entered.

"What do you want?" Jade asked.

"I want to sleep over here. They are already asleep over in the boring tent."

"Fine," Tabby said. "Just don't make this the interesting tent."

Sara glared at her as she came in and placed herself between Michelle and William.

"What the fuck are you doing?" Jade asked. I don't want you sleeping next to him."

"Oh but you don't mind Michelle sleeping next to him?" Sara countered.

"Hey, don't get me involved in your quarrel," Michelle said.

"Michelle wouldn't try to steal him from me," Jade said.

"Neither would I," Sara smiled. "Unless he wanted to be stole from you."

'She's right,' Jade thought. *'I don't want to be with someone who doesn't want me and only me. Let's test him.'* "Okay," Jade said.

"What?" William asked in shock.

"I said okay," Jade repeated. "She can sleep next to you. I trust you."

Sara was equally shocked. She took pleasure in pissing Jade off but Jade no longer seemed pissed.

"I'm going to sleep," Tabby said. She was sick of all their little head games. Michelle was sleeping at this time as well.

"Looks like just the three of us," Sara said with her evil grin. "What ya wanna do?"

"I'm going to make out with my man," Jade said. "I don't know what you're going to do." Jade wrapped her arms around William and began to kiss him.

'Great,' Sara thought. *'I know he won't have anything to do with me if she's already messing around with him. She's starting to play this game pretty smart.'* Sara got discouraged and turned to go to sleep.

17

The morning came and Sara was the first to wake. She looked over to see William with his arm around Jade. Jade's head was peacefully resting on William's chest. Sara slid over and mimicked Jade's position, placing her head on William's chest. He instinctively wrapped his arm around her. Sara's face was now inches from Jade's as they faced each other. She relaxed and waited for Jade to wake. She knew this would definitely piss her off. Sara placed her face as close to Jade's as she could without touching it. It was so close that two eyes would look as one. Then she stared and waited.

Jade woke up and was startled by Sara being in front of her. Sara quickly kissed her on the lips.

"What the fuck are you doing?" Jade yelled. The others began to wake from her outburst. Jade stood up as Sara still lay on William's chest. "Get up bitch!" Jade yelled. William had a look of horror on his face as he lowered his arm off Sara's shoulder.

"No thanks," Sara said with her devilish grin. "I'm more comfy right here," she said as she snuggled with William. Jade reached down and grabbed Sara's arm and pulled her to her feet. Tabby and Michelle quickly left the tent. Jade punched Sara in the stomach as William quickly rose to his feet. Sara clutched her stomach and dropped to one knee. William went over and tried to hold Jade back but she shoved him off. As Jade approached Sara again, Sara stood up and punched Jade on her cheek right below her left eye. Jade stumbled backwards as O'Dell entered and grabbed her. Sara was grinning from ear to ear despite the immense pain in her stomach. Jade was still noticeable angry. Her left eye was developing a little bruise under it.

"You two need to knock it off!" O'Dell yelled. Jade shook Michael off and went outside. William followed her. The plains were empty except for an Ankylosaurus that was about a hundred feet away eating the lush green grass. William walked over to Jade and put his arm around her.

"Jade, I love you," he said. "I would never do anything with Sara."

"I know," she said somberly. "She just finds ways to really annoy me. I'm sorry for fighting."

"You need to be able to control your anger. If there were Raptors or a T-Rex near by you would have drawn them right toward us."

"I know," Jade said as she lowered her head into her hands and began to cry. The light pressure of her hands started her head aching. William wrapped his arms around her and held her tight.

Sara and O'Dell walked out of the tent. Sara was still grinning from ear to ear. She was proud of herself. She had just fought with the World Kickboxing Champion and held her own. She wasn't kidding herself though. She was also happy that O'Dell broke it up when he did.

She had planned it that way. She knew there would be a fight. All she had to do was hold her own until someone broke it up. Everyone picked up the tents and began their journey back to the ship. William was by Jade's side the whole way home.

Chapter Fifteen:
Gunallo

1

When they arrived to the field O'Dell signaled for everyone to get down. Past the ship on the far side of the field were two Raptors.

"Should we run for the ship?" Wesley asked.

"We would never make it," Tom said. "Michael, do you think you can make it to the ship to get the gun?"

"I can try to sneak to ship. Stay down," he said. O'Dell snuck through the field and into the ship. Everyone remained quiet as they crouched. Sara just happened to be crouched right next to Jade. She looked over at Jade with a grin. She nudged Jade with her shoulder. Jade quietly nudged her back. They got into a slight pushing match until William crawled over and stopped them. Jade stared at Sara filled with anger.

"Nice shiner," Sara said as she let out a giggle. Like a tight thread, Jade snapped. She dropped her spear and leaped on top of Sara. They began to trade punches and roll around. This got the Raptor's attention and they made a dead run toward the group. The Raptor's dewclaws were tearing up the dirt as they sprinted across the field. Jade and Sara continued to fight oblivious of the two Raptors. The first Raptor leaped at Kiya and she speared it in the throat. It dropped to the ground and kicked and squirmed. Coy grabbed Jade's spear and ended the Raptor's life. The second Raptor was headed for Sara and Jade, who were still rolling on the ground. William jumped in front of Jade and Sara to block the Raptor. It was now headed for him. He put his hands up and closed his eyes as it drew near. A shot rang out and the Raptor dropped. William opened his eyes to see O'Dell standing outside the ship with the gun. O'Dell began to run toward them. The fighting had stopped now and Coy pulled Jade up off of Sara. They were both bloody and battered. They stood there upset at themselves. They knew that they had screwed up big this time.

2

"What the fuck is going on?" O'Dell yelled as he approached. "You two damn near cost William his life."

"I'm sorry," Jade said. "You're right. We should have never put you guys in danger."

"This has to end," William said.

"Gunallo," Kiya said.

"What?" William asked.

"It is forbidden by my people to fight among each other," Kiya said. "There are too many enemies out here to make your friends enemies too. When two Dambroo fight we make them go to Gunallo."

"What is Gunallo?" William asked.

"It is a place; a challenge… a punishment, sort of."

"I'll do it!" Jade said.

"Jade honey, you don't even know what this Gunallo is," William pleaded.

"I don't care. I put you and the others at harm. I feel like shit for doing that. This is the only way I know how to ask for forgiveness."

"I'll do it too," Sara added.

"Okay," O'Dell said. "Kiya, where is this Gunallo?"

"The entrance is in my village. The exit is far from there and not always found."

"What do you mean not always found?" William asked with concern.

"Some people can't get over their differences. If you can't overcome your hatred for each other, there is no way out."

"Jade are you sure about this?" William asked in doubt. He knew how much Jade despised Sara.

"Yes, it is something I have to do to feel better about my place on this mission."

"Well, let's go to the Dambroo village then," Michael suggested.

3

They began walking to the village. Jade's face was in pain. Her lip was split and there were a couple bruises. Now that the adrenaline of fighting was gone, the pain from the results set in. She looked to her left at Sara who was walking silently next to her. Sara had dried blood under her nose and black eye. There was also a cut above her eyebrow. *For a rich, spoiled, pretty girl, she can hold her own in a fight,'* Jade thought. Jade would never admit this to Sara. She would never hear the end of it if she did. It was here and now though that she admitted it to herself.

Sara was also in immense pain though. She knew she would be but didn't care. She wanted Jade to also know that she wasn't afraid of her. Even if she got her ass kicked it would be a moral victory to show Jade she wasn't afraid. She hadn't gotten her ass kicked though. It was a relatively even fight which made her even more happy.

When they all arrived at the Dambroo village they split up. Kiya went to see Queen Laza while the others went to Jango's house. Kiya explained to Queen Laza about Sara and Jade and the queen agreed that Gunallo was appropriate. It was starting to get late and nobody should have to face the Gunallo at night so the queen suggested they wait until morning. Kiya returned to the others at Jango's hut. She told them the news and everyone turned in. The explorers slept on Jango's floor. Sara slept on one end and Jade and William were on the other side of the room.

4

When the morning came Sara and Jade said their goodbyes. William and Kiya went with them to see the queen. When they arrived at Queen Laza's throne two guards approached them. Kiya introduced everyone to them. The tall, muscular guard with black hair was named Mikano. The short, cheerful, brunette guard was named Matuni, but everyone called him Tuni for short.

Tuni and Mikano led Kiya and the others to a door behind the queen's throne. Queen Laza gave a good luck nod as they entered. Inside the door was a tunnel. There were two torches on the wall. Mikano and Tuni each grabbed one and led them down the corridor. The ground sloped slightly down. The six of them walked in near silence for two hours.

'What did I get myself into?' Sara thought. Finally they had reached a door at the end of the tunnel. To the left there was a ladder leading up into the darkness.

'I wonder how far up that goes,' Sara thought.

"Okay, I'm going to explain this," Kiya said. "William and I will wait at the top for you." They opened the door and entered the bottom of a giant pit. The top of the pit was at least a hundred feet up.

"I think I have second thoughts," William said. "They can't do this."

"Yes they can," Kiya insisted. The pit was fifty feet wide. The walls to the east and west were straight, unclimbable rock. The wall to the north was about fifty feet high with a ledge on top. There were blades sticking out of the rock wall about six inches. They each had upward hooks at their ends. They were spaced about three feet apart all the way up the rock wall. The south wall had the same blade setup but must have been a hundred feet high until there was a large ledge. The wall continued up from there for another hundred feet.

5

Mikano went over to a box by the wall. He opened it and pulled out two sets of locking metal rings. He placed one around Jade's left wrist and checked to see if it was snug. This was the Dambroo form of handcuffs. Then he cuffed the other one to Sara's right wrist. A foot long chain that linked the rings now connected them.

"I have to be cuffed to her?" Sara asked.

"Yes," Kiya answered. "This is how this works. There are three keys in the Gunallo. You must find all three before you leave. It will take courage and teamwork."

Tuni placed the other set of rings around their legs.

"Our legs have to be connected to each other too?" Jade complained.

"Yes," Kiya answered. "There is a key for your hands, a key for your legs, and a key for the door at the top of Gunallo. Good luck." William gave Jade a kiss and left with Kiya, Tuni, and Mikano. They exited the door they entered and locked it.

"Great! What do we do now?" Sara asked.

"Look around for a key," Jade replied. Sara began to walk left as Jade walked right. The sudden jerk from their ankles quickly stopped them.

"Alright," Jade said. "As much as I hate you, I hate this place more. We need to work together." They circled around the Gunallo floor looking for a key. The chains allowed for some movement but not much. After circling for a while they stopped looking on the ground.

6

"I think we have to climb," Jade suggested.

"Okay," Sara agreed. "The door is obviously at the top of the high cliff so we should climb that."

"No, I don't think so," Jade said.

"What do you mean no? Don't you want out of here?"

"Kiya said that there were three keys. I don't think that they would put all three in the same place. The door has got to be at the top but I would hate to get there without all three keys."

"You're right," Sara said. "We should climb the short cliff and check on top of the ledge."

They walked over to the fifty-foot wall. Sara touched one of the blades sticking out.

"These things are sharp as hell!" she stated. "How are we going to climb this? There's no handholds or ledges. It's straight rock face except for these blades and they'll cut us to shreds."

"They won't cut the chains," Jade said with a smile.

"You want us to climb up a fifty foot cliff using only these chains?" Sara asked.

"That's exactly what we're going to do," Jade replied.

"You're fucking crazy! How are we going to do that?"

"Just do exactly what I do," Jade said as she raised her left arm up. Sara raised her right arm and they looped the chain from the cuffs over one of the blades. "Now grab the chain with your hand so you don't hurt your wrist," Jade suggested. They both grabbed the chain with their hand. "Now, we are going to pull ourselves up and loop our ankle chain on the bottom blade."

"Won't that hurt our calves and ankles?" Sara asked.

"Yeah," Jade replied. "But it's the only way up. We have to work together. If you pull at a different time than I do we could be in big trouble."

Sara was doubtful that this would work. She didn't however have a better idea so she decided to try this.

"Are you ready?" Jade asked.

"I guess so," Sara said unenthusiastically.

"Okay, one, two, three, pull!"

They both pulled up with their arms and looped their ankle chain on top of the bottom blade. The chain was off center and they fell to the ground.

"Great idea," Sara said.

"It's the only way up," Jade insisted.

"There's no way, Jade. It's impossible."

"No it's not, but I need you to help me. Come on, we can do it."

They stood up and prepared to try again.

"Ready," Jade asked and Sara nodded. They looped their wrist chain around the blade and pulled themselves up. They placed the ankle chain on the bottom blade evenly. They relieved the pressure from their arms and all their weight was now on their ankle chain.

"This hurts," Sara said.

"Stop whining. I have to deal with it too."

"Yeah, but you weigh more than me," Sara said. "So it's your fault it hurts so much."

"Sara, we need to stop arguing and get through this. We need to put the weight back on our arms and lift our feet to the next blade. Then we can stand and raise our arms to the next one."

"Okay," Sara agreed. As they pulled up, the chain connecting their wrists slid down the blade until it caught the hook at the end. They pulled themselves up and placed their ankle chain on the next blade. There was a wobble but they held firm and didn't fall. They continued up the wall, each on opposite sides of the blades. They moved as one. Their biceps were becoming more tired and the red marks on their ankles were getting darker and darker. When they reached the top blade they could see a rod sticking up on top of the ledge. They lassoed it with their wrist chain and pulled themselves up. They collapsed on the ledge and were motionless for a while.

7

While laying on the ledge, exhausted and pain ridden, they looked around. The ledge was about fifteen wide by twenty-five feet long. There was another rod at the other end of the ledge. On the ground was a little spike with a shiny silver key attached by rope. Their exhaustion ceased as they ran over together and Jade grabbed the key. She tried it in the ankle cuffs first. Their ankles were getting raw from the rubbing cuffs. The key worked! She handed it to Sara who unlocked her ankle as well. The relief of having those cuffs off was tremendous. Their ankles burned as the cool air blew over them. Sara tried the key in her wrist cuffs but it didn't fit. They lay there and rested for about a half-hour. After that, Jade got up and dragged Sara with her to the other edge of the ledge. When she looked down she noticed another key on a spike hanging on the rock wall. It was down about eight feet from the top.

"I found another key," Jade said blandly.

"Great, get it," Sara replied.

"It's not that simple. It's down a ways and there are no blades sticking out."

Sara looked down with her at the key. "How are we going to get that?" she asked.

Jade tried to think as she looked intently at the pole sticking out of the ground. "Give me the ankle key," Jade said.

"Why? We don't need it anymore."

"I need it," Jade replied.

"Fine," Sara said as she handed Jade the key. Jade tucked it into her shoe for safekeeping. Then, she put both ankle cuffs on her ankles and latched them.

"What the hell are you doing?" Sara asked.

"I'm getting the key, but I need your help."

"What do I have to do?" Sara asked.

"You'll see," Jade said with a smile. She sat with her back to the edge and looped the ankle chain around the pole, which was about three feet from the edge of the ledge. "Okay, I'm going to dangle over the edge. I need you to go with me to get the key."

"You're crazy!" Sara yelled. "I'll fall."

"How will you fall, moron? You're cuffed to my wrist!"

"You can't hold my weight," Sara said.

"Sure I can. You're the light one remember." Jade sat on the ledge with her back to the edge. "Now I need you to lay on top of me facing the opposite direction and hug me," Jade said.

"What?" Sara asked.

"Just do it!" Jade yelled as she leaned back. Sara reluctantly placed her knees on each side of Jade's head. She leaned down and reluctantly put her head on Jade's stomach. Jade turned her head sideways to allow Sara's stomach to touch her cheek. "Okay, now hang on to me. I'm going to slide off the ledge."

"Are you fucking crazy? What if the pole doesn't hold?" Sara asked.

"Well then, I guess we're fucked," Jade said as she scooted off the ledge with Sara holding her. They fell until the ankle chains caught the pole. Sara was holding on tightly but the sudden stop made her lose her grip. She fell off Jade but was suddenly stopped by the wrist cuffs. The pull sent pain shooting through Jade's shoulder. All of Sara's weight was pulling down on Jade's wrist. The pain was excruciating. Sara hung there with her eyes closed in fear.

"Well," Jade said. "Get the fucking key! This isn't fun you know!"

"Hold on, I'll get it!" Sara reached down and grabbed the key. She pulled herself back up and latched onto Jade. The tension was now off their wrists but the pain was still there.

"Put your foot on the spike and help push me up," Jade said.

Sara supported her weight with the spike. She leaned back off of Jade as Jade tried to lean up. Just when Jade got her head up past her waist Sara's foot slipped. She fell as the cuffs yanked Jade backward and her head smacked the rock wall. Her shoulder and wrist were now feeling the pain of supporting Sara again. That was momentarily outweighed by the pain her head currently felt from smashing against the rock wall.

"What the hell are you doing?" Jade yelled.

"I slipped," Sara responded. "Sorry."

"I'd let go of you if I could."

"You need me as much as I need you and you know it, Jade!"

"Well you're not helping right now. Climb back up and put your foot on the spike."

Sara climbed Jade's body until she could place her foot on the blade that stuck out of the rock wall. Jade's head was throbbing as she tried to sit up again. Sara put her hands on Jade's back and shoulders and guided her up until her head was by her knees.

"I need you to help push my ass up to the ledge," Jade said. "Can you do that?"

"I think so," Sara replied. "Just keep your hand close to mine so you don't jerk my hand away with the cuffs."

"Ok."

Sara put her hands on Jade's butt and began to push her up. Jade pulled with her legs. Just before Sara pushed Jade up onto the ledge she gave her butt a little squeeze.

"What the hell?" Jade yelled.

"I'm just joking around. Chill out."

Jade slid up on the ledge, turned and pulled Sara up with her. Jade collapsed on the ledge and began panting from exhaustion.

8

"How come you can't relax and have a good time?" Sara asked. "You can't even joke around."

Jade looked at her in shock. "What the hell are you talking about? We were suspended upside-down, fifty feet above the ground. Not to mention, all of your weight was hanging on my wrist by these stupid fucking cuffs. But you want me to relax and have a good time. Are you fucking serious?"

"Okay, I see your point," Sara said. "But even when we're not in danger you don't relax and enjoy life."

"Out here we're always in danger. My goal is to stay alive. If I succeed, then I will enjoy life."

"Fine," Sara said. "But you don't have to be so grouchy. Have some fun."

"I don't like you. Why do you want me to have fun?"

"It will be more fun for everyone if you're in a good mood," Sara explained.

"Alright!" Jade yelled. "Stop nagging me. I'll try."

"Great!" Sara yelled cheerfully. "Now give me a hug!"

Jade looked over in disbelief. "That's not happening."

"Yes it is," Sara said. "If you want me to help you get out of this pit then I want a hug."

"Fine," Jade said as she hesitantly wrapped her arms around Sara.

"Now was that so hard?"

"Unpleasant is more like it," Jade said.

9

Sara pulled the key out and tried it in her wrist cuffs. It worked. "Yes!" she cheered as she handed the key to Jade. Jade unlocked her wrist and then used the other key to unlock her ankles. They rested for a while on the ledge.

"Only one more key," Sara said.

Jade nodded. "We have to put the cuffs back on to get down you know."

"I know," Sara said.

They decided to switch so the cuffs would be on fresh ankles and wrists. With their raw ankles and wrist getting a break they started their descent. When they safely reached the bottom, they unlocked themselves and walked around for a while. Jade began to look up at the enormous cliff that she knew they had to climb. It was so painful to climb the other cliff and that was half the height of this one. Her muscles were sore. She could only imagine how sore Sara's were. Jade was a well-trained kick boxer and Sara was a rich, spoiled girl. Jade seemed to be the one in pain though. If Sara's muscles were hurting she hid it well. Jade respected her for this.

10

Sara joined her at the bottom of the large rock wall.

"That's gonna be tough," Sara said.

"I know," Jade answered. "When we start we have to put everything into it. We have to be on the same page. We have to endure the pain."

"We can do it," Sara said confidently. "I'll take comfort knowing that the pain I'm going through is being felt by you as well. We can do it together."

"Okay," Jade said. "I'll need your full effort on this."

"I'll be right there beside you," Sara answered with a smile.

Jade was inspired. She thought she would have to pull this little rich girl along like dead weight. Instead it was Sara's seemingly absence of pain and positive outlook that fueled Jade.

"We will move as one," Jade said as she smiled back at Sara. They began their climb using the cuffs and blades.

It wasn't long before their ankles and wrists felt as bad as the others. Halfway up Sara stopped.

"What's wrong," Jade asked.

"It hurts," Sara replied. "I can't do it."

"I know it hurts. I need you. Fight through it. We can do it. It will hurt just as bad to go back down as it will to climb up the rest of the way."

"You're right," Sara said.

"If we make it to the top I'll give you a huge hug. Hell, I might even kiss you."

Sara began to laugh. "Alright, let's go!" After another hour, they collapsed at the top.

"We did it!" Sara yelled.

"Yes we did," Jade said with a smile. She unlocked the ankle and wrist cuffs. There was another key suspended on a pole. Jade crawled over to it and grabbed it. A few feet away was a door in the cliff wall

"Is that the key for the door?" Sara asked.

"I believe so," Jade answered.

"Jade, I couldn't have done this without you pushing me all the way."

"Well I needed your positive attitude to get me through," Jade replied.

"Hey," Sara said. "I'm sorry for all the trouble I've caused."

"That's water under the bridge now." They got up and Jade hugged Sara. "I'll try to loosen up and have more fun from now on."

"I'll stay away from William," Sara said. "I want you two to be happy."

"You don't have to stay away, just be a friend. That's all I ask."

"After this I do feel like your friend," Sara said. "We experienced something out here that was so terrible, but experiencing it together made it so beautiful. No matter how hard we try to explain it to the others they will never understand."

"If you ever need anything, I'm here for you," Jade said.

"Likewise," Sara replied.

11

They walked together over to the door and unlocked it. They opened it to see Kiya and William sitting in a small room waiting for them.

"You did it!" William yelled as he rushed to Jade and hugged her.

"No," Jade said. "We did it." Kiya went over and hugged Sara. Kiya was startled as Jade hugged her next. William was cautious about hugging Sara. He didn't want to make Jade jealous. Jade could see he wanted to hug her.

"Go ahead," she said. "It's okay." William hugged Sara tightly as he was overjoyed by the apparently new attitudes of both Sara and Jade.

"Oh my god, your ankles," William said as he looked over to Jade's raw ankles.

"It's okay. It was worth it," Jade said.

"Yes, definitely worth it," Sara added. "Thank you Kiya."

Kiya smiled as they all climbed down the ladder to the tunnel that entered Gunallo on one end and the Dambroo village on the other.

Chapter Sixteen:
Relaxation

1

Kiya opened the door and they entered the Dambroo village from behind Queen Laza's throne. She was not there but many of the Dambroo were gathered and waiting for their return. They began to cheer for Jade and Sara. Everyone was approaching them and congratulating them as they walked toward Jango's hut.

Back at Jango's hut the others could hear the cheering.

"What is all that noise?" Michelle asked.

Jango stood up and said, "Compinyon mon damyu ena umph!" Then he ran out of the hut with a grin on his face.

"They have returned," Tabitha translated. Her and the others walked outside to see Jade and Sara walking toward them, followed by Kiya and William. Jade and Sara took turns hugging everyone from their crew and Jango as well.

Tabitha didn't understand why Jade was hugging everyone. This was not at all like Jade. Jade was a distant person who was not very affectionate.

"What the hell was that all about,"

"I don't know but I'm not complaining. Jade is actually smiling for once," Michelle said.

"Now that you have been welcomed back, you must see Queen Laza," Kiya said. They all went to the throne where the queen had returned. She was surrounded by Tuni, Mikano, and two other guards. The guards all quickly left. "As customary, the queen would like to offer you a gift," Kiya stated. "Everyone who survives Gunallo is truly a warrior and should be rewarded."

2

The guards returned now carrying a large pot. Each guard had a wooden pole on his shoulder that supported the large pot. Two guards walked in front of the pot and two in back.

"Dako," Sara said. "What is it?" she asked Kiya.

"It's a water pot. Go look inside."

Sara and Jade walked over to the pot as the guards lowered it to the ground. Inside were several drawings and paintings. Each one depicted Sara and Jade in Gunallo.

"Every child in the village has drawn their version of the mighty warriors Sara and Jade as they fought together through Gunallo," Kiya explained.

"That is so sweet," Jade said as a tear ran down her face. It felt good. She felt good about herself again. The others would not understand the feeling one gets after Gunallo but Jade didn't care. She did it to prove that she was wrong for fighting and to prove her place in the mission. It ended up having more significance than that though. Her and Sara had quickly changed from hated enemies to loving friends. That is what the others wouldn't understand and Jade didn't care. She could now trust Sara with her life and likewise Sara could trust her.

"Is it okay for me to hug Queen Laza?" Sara asked.

"Yes," Kiya said as Jade and Sara together hugged and thanked the queen.

"This is marvelous," Tom said. "Now we don't have to get water as often."

"Yeah, but who's going to lug that big thing home?" Tabby asked. Coy, Wesley, William, and O'Dell volunteered. Everyone thanked Queen Laza for the pot and Jango for his hospitality. Then, they all headed home. The weight of the pot wasn't too bad with four people carrying it. It was a little hard to maneuver through the forest though. It was late when they returned home so everyone went to bed. Jade and Sara fell quickly asleep from their exhausting day. The others weren't far behind them.

The next morning came and Simonson asked for volunteers to get water with the new pot.

"I'll go," Sara said. "But I want to take a swim. Do we need the water right away or do I have time to swim while I'm there?"

"Oh no, you have time," Simonson said.

"We'll go too," Jade said referring to her and William.

"Heck, why don't we all go?" Coy suggested.

"No, I'm gonna go hunting," O'Dell said. Tom also decided to stay behind.

3

Michelle, Tabitha, Jade, and William all carried the pot. Sara, Coy, Kiya, and Wesley joined them as they all headed for the stream.

As they walked through the forest, Kiya stopped them. She heard a sound. It was the light crunching of branches underfoot. She and Coy raised the spears they were carrying.

"Monogatai," Kiya said.

"What's a Monogatai?" Wesley asked.

"Apemen," Kiya replied.

Two apemen walked out of the forest in front of them on the path. They were unaware of the group and were shocked when they saw the explorers. They noticed they were outnumbered and wisely walked off. At this point everyone switched spots. Sara, Coy, Wesley, and Kiya carried the pot now. They arrived at the stream and quickly filled the pot. Now, it was heavy.

4

Sara walked over to Jade and whispered in her ear. "I'm not getting my underwear wet and walking all the way back to camp in wet panties. I'm skinny dipping."

"What?" Jade said shocked.

"Come on, join me so I'm not the only one."

"You're crazy!" Jade said with a smile.

"So be crazy with me."

The Enchanted Planet

Jade thought about it for a moment: *'This is something that high school girls would do. It is completely irresponsible and immature...but fun!'* Her mind was made up.

"All right, but I'm making William do it too," Jade said. Jade walked over to William and asked him to go skinny-dipping with them. He started laughing because he didn't believe her. It was the playful, unwavering look on her face that made him realize that she was serious.

"It won't bother you if I'm naked in the water next to Sara?" he asked.

"I'll be right there with you guys. Besides, she won't try anything."

"Jade!" Sara called from behind a large bush. Jade ran over to her. Sara was already naked. The others were stripping down to their underwear. Jade joined Sara by becoming naked as well. "How do we get in without anyone seeing?" Jade asked.

"Who cares," Sara replied. "Let's just run for it."

William was watching with interest. He knew exactly what was about to happen and his eyes were glued to that bush waiting for the girls to step out. Sara and Jade ran to the water and jumped in. William caught a glimpse of Sara's nakedness. He had seen Jade once before in the one time they had been intimate while fetching water.

"Are you guys naked?" Tabitha asked as she looked over to Jade and Sara in the water. She knew the answer but was in disbelief.

"Yeah," Sara replied laughing a little.

"We don't want to wear wet underwear back to camp," Jade added.

"Besides, we're like family. I don't care if you see me naked," Sara said.

"Well I don't exactly want to wear wet underwear either," Michelle said. "And you guys have all seen me naked already."

"I haven't," Coy chimed in.

"Coy, shush!" Wesley snapped.

"Oh yeah, you weren't there were you," Michelle said. "Well, I guess it's your lucky day." Michelle removed the rest of her clothes and jumped into the water with Jade and Sara.

"Come on William," Jade persuaded. William took his boxers off and ran into the water.

"Oh why not," Kiya said as she stripped and walked gracefully into the water. William stared at her tan, well-toned body. He loved this. He was in the water with four beautiful naked women.

"Alright!" Wesley said as he joined them in the naked swim party.

"Come on Tabby," Michelle coaxed.

"Get real," Tabitha replied.

"Coy?" Sara asked.

"I guess so," he said. He disrobed and entered the comforting water. Now only Tabby stood out of the water with her underwear on.

"Please Tabby?" Michelle pleaded.

"Only if you all turn around."

"Fine," Sara said as they all turned their backs except William. He was under water at the moment and didn't hear a thing. He surfaced as Tabitha's naked body was walking toward the water.

"Hey," Tabby yelled as she jumped in.

"What?" William asked.

"No one was supposed to see," Tabitha said.

"Oh, sorry. I didn't hear that. You have nothing to be ashamed of," William said.

5

Jade came over to William and wrapped her arms around him. "Are you having a good time?" she asked.

"Yes. The old Jade would have never allowed this. You would have been pissed."

"Do you love me?" she asked.

"Of course," he answered.

"Well that's all that matters. I trust you."

"You guys are just like family to me," Michelle said. "Tom and Tabby have always been like family to me, but you guys are too."

"Even me?" Kiya asked.

"Yes, of course even you," Michelle answered. "Kiya, you have been so helpful to us. I don't know if we would even be alive still if it weren't for you."

"You're right Michelle," Sara said. "We are like family. Group hug!"

"Oh hell no!" Tabitha interjected.

"I was only kidding," Sara said as everyone began laughing.

"Coy are you having a good time?" Sara asked.

"I guess so," he answered plainly.

"I guess so? You have five naked women in the water with you."

"Well, sure. You guys are fun to look at, but you're my friends."

"Spoken like a true gentleman," Michelle said as she exited the water.

"We know that you're having a good time," Sara said to William.

"What do you mean?" he panicked. "You can't see underwater can you?"

Sara started laughing. "No silly. I mean we know what you're like."

Jade reached down and felt him. "Yeah, he's having a good time."

"Jade!" William objected as his face turned red.

"Sorry sweetie, I couldn't resist."

"Well, I'm having a blast!" Wesley added.

"Worth staying awake for huh," Sara said.

"I don't sleep that much."

"I don't think I'll sleep as much as you until I'm dead," Sara replied.

6

Tabitha was more relaxed now as she exited the water slowly.

"Tabby, you sex kitten," Sara yelled.

"What?"

"And you were afraid to show your body? You look good," Sara said.

"Thanks I guess," Tabby replied.

"Okay," Jade said to Sara. "You're scaring me."

"Oh Jade, you know you'll always be my favorite," Sara said as she hugged Jade.

"Knock it off," Jade said as she giggled. William could not believe the new playful Jade. He was extremely happy and welcomed the pleasant change. This was the most relaxed the explorers had been since they arrived on this planet.

Coy was the next to exit the water.

"Coy, how come you're not excited?" Sara jokingly asked.

"Um, I was. But then I just thought of what Professor Simonson would look like naked and that made it go away."

"Gross dude!" Wesley yelled as everyone started to chuckle.

"What?" Coy asked. "I'm serious."

Kiya exited the water next and began to get dressed with Coy. Michelle and Tabitha were dressed at this point.

"You're right Coy," Wesley said as he got out. "That does work." Sara and Jade began to get out as well.

"Come on William," Sara said as she grabbed his hand.

"Uh, I think I'm going to wait a minute," he replied.

"Let things calm down a little bit," Jade said as her and Sara began laughing. William gave them an angry glare.

"Tom naked didn't work for you huh," Wesley said. "I don't know if that's a bad thing or a really bad thing."

"Ha-ha, very funny," William said.

"Need help sweet cheeks?" Wesley asked as Sara and Jade made it to shore.

"Never gonna happen Wes," Sara replied.

"Can't blame me for trying. At least I got to see why I call you sweet cheeks."

William stepped out a few minutes later when everyone was dressed.

7

They took turns carrying the heavy pot of water until they made it to the field. There was something cooking over the fire pit.

"What is it?" William asked.

"I hope it's a deer," Jade replied. "I'm sick of Compy." When they arrived at the camp Tom stood by the fire cooking meat from a deer. The skin was lying on the ground.

"Yes!" Jade cheered. "Good job Michael," she yelled into the ship.

"Did you all enjoy your swim?" Tom asked.

"Oh yes, it was very…exciting," Sara said as she looked over to William. Her and Jade began giggling. William shrugged and went inside.

"Well, enjoy today," Simonson said. "We're traveling east tomorrow."

"East?" Michelle asked.

"Yes east," Tom replied.

"But we already know that the Pocala tribe is in the east past the Guanco Jaballa."

"No, I mean farther east, past the Great Desert and past the Pocala tribe."

"But that is the Shondo Waxanadu," Kiya said.

"And what does that mean?" Tom asked.

"Forbidden Swamp. The Dambroo have been forbidden to go there."

"Well you don't have to go if you don't want to but I still want to go. We need to find a way off of this planet."

"I'll go," Kiya said. "You will need rafts. We can borrow some from my village, but we better keep our voyage silent."

"Will we be able to get the rafts we need?" Tom asked.

"We will probably need three rafts," Kiya said. "I can get Jango's, Tuni's, and maybe Kolani's."

"Who are Tuni and Kolani?" Tom asked.

"Tuni is a guard," Sara piped in.

"Yes, and Kolani is what Americans call a cousin to Jango. He would probably let us borrow his raft also."

"Great!" Tom said.

"Why are we doing all this exploring?" Coy asked. "It seems dangerous."

"Well, we are hopefully going to find someone who can give us some fuel for the ship. It is dangerous, but we are in danger the longer we are on this planet. We have to do whatever we can to find help," Tom explained. "We leave early in the morning." Everyone relaxed for the rest of the day and packed that night for their adventure in the morning.

Chapter Seventeen:
Shondo Waxanadu

1

The next morning everyone grabbed the tents and headed east to the Dambroo village. Michael carried the gun. Jade, Kiya, and Tabby each had spears. Coy and William carried the tent packs.

"So Kiya, what do you know about this swamp?" Michelle asked.

"Not much. All I know are stories of the Makai."

"What are the Makai?' Michelle asked.

"They are just a legend that my people created to keep us out of the swamp. They are supposed to be like the Monogatai or as you say apemen. But they are said to be more agile and smarter. Legend has it that they protect the swamp from all other tribes. They live in the treetops and move by vines. They use sleeping darts to stop people from entering the swamp."

"They sound similar to monkeys, but with some human traits," Tom said.

"Tabby has explained to me what a monkey is. They are the ones used in the kur-sus right?"

"Circus," Tabby said. "I can't believe you remember that talk."

"I got the word wrong though didn't I?" Kiya asked.

"Yes, but that is the creature we are talking about."

"I have never seen anything like what you call a monkey. The only thing close I've seen is the Monogatai. The Makai sound similar I guess, but I have never seen a Makai."

"Maybe long ago there were monkeys here and that is where your tribes story originated," Tom suggested. "Most myths and legends have some truth to them."

"Maybe, I don't know," Kiya replied. "Like I said, it is forbidden for the Dambroo to go there."

2

When they arrived at the Dambroo village, the guards welcomed them. Kiya led everyone to Tuni's hut. He was outside when they arrived. Kiya spoke to him in Dambroo for a few minutes. Then she walked over and grabbed his raft from the side of his hut.

"Dako," she said.

"Sarto kai," he replied.

They followed her to Kolani's hut next. He was in his garden when they arrived. He also agreed to let them use his raft.

"Dako," everyone said.

"Your welcome," Kolani answered to everyone's surprise. "Jango sono," Kolani said.

"What does sono mean?" Michelle asked Tabby.

"Teach," Tabitha said. "Jango taught him your welcome."

They left Kolani's and went to Jango's next. When Kiya asked Jango to borrow his raft he responded proudly in English.

"Where going?" he asked.

"Shondo Waxanadu," Sara replied as Jango's eyes grew large in fright. Kiya shook her head in disbelief that Sara told him after she was reminded that Shondo Waxanadu was a forbidden place. As soon as it came out Sara knew she had done wrong. Jango began yelling at Kiya in Dambroo. Kiya tried to explain the situation to Jango.

"What's going on?" Sara asked Tabitha.

"He doesn't want her to go," Tabby explained. "He says it's forbidden and she should respect the Dambroo rules. Kiya is asking him if he believed in the legend. Jango doesn't believe in the legend but wants to know for sure. He refuses to let her go unless he goes too."

"Okay," Kiya said. After Jango led everyone outside to his raft, they all walked toward the doors of the village.

Kiya walked over to Sara. "I told you not to tell anyone where we were going."

"I know," Sara said. "I'm sorry."

"It's okay. Since living with you guys I've missed Jango. It will be nice to spend some time with him."

3

They left the village and continued east. By the time the suns were in the center of the sky they had reached the great dessert. They walked through the dessert until it started getting dark. They stopped for the night and Coy showed Jango how to set up the tents. Jango watched with interest as Coy guided the support rods into the proper sleeves. After the tents were up everyone went in and settled down. In the first tent was Tom, Wesley, Michael, Coy, Kiya, and Jango. It was a little tight with six but they were in for a chilly night so it would help in the long run. The other tent hosted Michelle, Tabby, Sara, William, and Jade. Tom, O'Dell, and Wesley were fast asleep. Kiya and Jango stayed up talking in Dambroo. Coy was up for a while but felt left out and went to bed.

In the other tent everyone was awake talking.

"So William, did you enjoy swimming yesterday?" Tabby asked.

"Yes. You guys made it very interesting."

"I thought it was interesting to see the girl's bodies," Michelle said as everyone gave her an odd look. "No, not like that. I mean, I knew Jade would be well put together but I was a little surprised at how well toned Kiya was."

"What did you expect," Sara said. "She has been living out here, running from Raptors and fighting off cannibals and apemen. We've taken our planet for granted. Sure we have murders and crime, but out here every day your goal is to stay alive. On Earth, I'm pretty much set because I have money but out here that means nothing."

"It is pretty tough out here," Michelle said. "We definitely would struggle without each other."

"What did you think about Kiya's body, William?" Jade asked.

"I thought we were off that subject already," he answered.

"Relax," Jade said. "I don't care. I'm just curious."

"Well then, her body was really nice," he said with a smile.

4

Everyone decided to turn in but the air was quite chilly. Michelle and Tabitha were cuddling to stay warm, as were Jade and William.

Sara was left out. Michelle and Tabby were fast asleep when Jade called over. "Sara," she whispered.

"Wh… Wh… what?" Sara asked as the chill caused her stutter.

"Are you cold?"

"Ye…yes."

"Come cuddle with us," Jade suggested.

"Jade!" William snapped.

"What?"

"This is the same girl you hated for even touching me. Now you want her to cuddle?" he asked.

"Yes. Sara and I are okay now. She's not going to try anything."

William gave Jade a look of doubt.

"Come on over here Sara."

"Are you su…sure?" Sara asked.

"Yes. I said if you ever needed anything to let me know. You need warmth so get your ass over here."

Sara came over and laid her head on William's chest with Jade's. He wrapped his arm around her.

5

The night passed and morning came. William woke up with Jade and Sara still clinging to him. Michelle and

Tabby had already left the tent. O'Dell was making a lot of noise as he and Coy tore down the other tent. William woke Sara and Jade. Sara woke and smiled at both Jade and William.

"Thanks for keeping me warm guys," she said.

"Anytime," Jade replied.

They got up and helped tear down their tent and the journey east continued. The explorers stayed a safe distance from the Pocala village as they went around.

"Want to go visit your friends, Michelle?" William joked.

"I'll pass, thanks," she replied.

Past the rocky plains was a forest. The forest became thicker the farther they walked. There were puddles of water throughout the forest. Vines hung down from the tall lush trees. It wasn't long before they were walking in an inch of water, which covered the ground. A thick layer of fog covered the water, which became deeper with every step. They walked until the water was almost waist deep.

6

"We are now in the Shondo Waxanadu," Kiya said. "We should get on the rafts now." The first raft carried Tabby, Michelle, Kiya, and Jango. Raft two hosted Jade, William, Sara, and Wesley. The last raft had Tom, Michael, and Coy on it. They slowly rowed through the fog, unable to see the treetops above or the water below.

Suddenly, Tabitha collapsed.

"Tabby," Michelle yelled as she noticed a little dart in the side of Tabby's neck. Michelle thought of the stories

Tabby had told her of tribes in the Amazon that would use Poison Arrow Frogs to coat their darts. They would use blowguns to fire the darts into their prey.

"Turn around!" Kiya yelled. Another dart hit William in the neck and dropped him onto Sara's lap.

"I thought you said the Makai were a legend, Kiya!" Michelle yelled.

"I thought they were!" Kiya responded. Michelle and Tom were both hit next with little darts.

"We're losing paddlers," O'Dell yelled as he looked toward the treetops but saw nothing except fog. "Hurry up!"

Michael and Coy made it safely out of the fog. Coy carried Tom, and Michael dragged the raft to safety. Michelle and Tabby were both unconscious on the front of their raft as Kiya and Jango paddled from the back. Suddenly a brown, monkeylike creature swung down toward them from a vine. The creature swung a machete as Kiya ducked. She turned around to see Jango's head fall into the water and his body fall lifelessly onto the raft. Kiya began to cry uncontrollably. Kiya paddled as hard as she could but the raft was far to heavy for her to go fast.

7

Michael and Coy awaited eagerly outside the Shondo Waxanadu for someone else to emerge from the fog. They saw a raft appearing. It was Jade, Sara, and Wesley, with William lying motionless. Coy ran over and grabbed William as Wesley pulled the raft to safety.

Kiya was still struggling to go faster as one of the Makai swooped down and swung at her with his machete.

She fell back onto Jango's body as the machete swooped just over her. She sat back up and continued to row.

"I'm sorry Jango," she said as she rolled his headless body into the water. "I loved you great friend." The raft began to move faster for her without his weight. She hated doing this. Jango deserved better, but she had two other people on the raft to worry about now. There was nothing more she could do for Jango.

Sara and Jade were checking on Tom and William who were still out cold. Through the edge of the fog the third raft was visible. Michael, Wesley, and Coy ran to the raft. They saw Tabby and Michelle lying on it. Kiya was rowing with all her might with her head down. Coy and Wesley pulled Tabitha and Michelle off and dragged them to safety.

"Where is Jango?' O'Dell asked.

"Gone," Kiya sobbed.

"Come on," he said as they pulled the raft up to the others.

"Are we safe out here?" Sara asked.

"According to the legend, the Makai only live in the swamp. We should be safe," Kiya said.

"What about William and the others?" Sara asked.

Kiya felt each of their necks for a pulse. "Just sleeping," Kiya said. "They were only sleeping darts. I believe the darts were dipped in the liquid from the Bufelesali plant. They should wake shortly. Michael pulled the little needle-like darts out of everyone. "They should wake shortly," Kiya said as she began to cry.

"Are you okay?" Sara asked.

"He was my best friend," Kiya said. "We went through Gunallo together."

"You had to go through Gunallo?" Jade asked.

"Yes. When Jango and I were young, maybe thirteen or fourteen in your Earth years, we got into a huge fight while we were being trained to hunt. We scared off the deer and alerted a T-Rex to our presence."

"Did anyone get hurt?" Jade asked.

"No, but Queen Laza was not happy when she found out. Children are supposed to have total discipline and respect. So, we were sent to Gunallo."

"I couldn't imagine," Sara said. "You were just kids and you had to endure Gunallo?"

"Yes, it hurt but we fought through it, Jango and I together. We were best friends."

"I'm sorry," Sara said as she hugged Kiya.

"I had to watch him die," Kiya said.

"I know how you feel. I had to watch my father die."

8

"What's going on," Tabitha asked as she woke up and felt her neck. Slowly William, Michelle, and Tom also woke up. "Where's Jango," Tabby asked.

"He didn't make it," O'Dell answered.

"I'm sorry," Tom said to Kiya. "What happened?"

"We were attacked by the Makai," Kiya answered.

"I think we should head back," Tom said. "There is certainly nothing to help us in the east."

The mood was dispiriting as everyone walked out of the forest and into the rocky plains. As they walked, there was something approaching from the distance. The explorers couldn't quite make out what it was at first. Then they saw the five Pocala warriors approaching them.

"Shit," O'Dell said. "This is not what we need." He raised his gun.

"Relax," Kiya said as her hand lowered the barrel of O'Dell's gun. "They only wanted Michelle for their sacrifice. That time has passed. Everyone relax and let them do their thing. We should be able to get out of this without conflict." One of the warriors approached them. He walked up to William and felt his face. Then, he went over to Kiya and felt her face.

"Dambroo?" he asked.

Kiya was a little shocked by the Pocala warrior's observation.

"Lano," Kiya said which is 'yes' in Dambroo. He examined Jade next. The warrior rambled off a sentence in Dambroo.

"He says you look like a warrior," Kiya interpreted.

"Dako," Jade said to him as he smiled.

He examined everyone one by one. Then he gently grabbed Tabitha's wrist and guided her a few steps forward. He did the same to Wesley and Michael.

"Pantoo?" he asked.

"Gula," Kiya answered which means 'no'.

"He thinks that we are cannibals?" Tabby asked.

"Yes," Kiya said. They are the only dark people on our planet.

"Damn," Wesley said. "Can you believe this shit? We are a million miles from Earth and we still can't avoid racism."

Tabitha laughed. "At least here it's because of being naïve and not hatred toward us." The Pocala warrior rejoined his tribesmen and they walked off.

"The Pocala speak Dambroo?" Tabby asked.

"That one does," Kiya answered. "He must have learned from one of our people that were held captive."

"Let's go home," Michelle suggested.

9

They made it halfway through the desert before they decided to make camp. Kiya walked away from the others. She found a spot on the sand and sat down. Jango's death was really bothering her. *'I'm sorry my friend,'* she thought. *'If you didn't know where we were going you would have given us your raft without questions. In fact, I should have borrowed someone else's raft. I'll miss you.'*

The tents were all set up. As usual, Tom, Michael, and Wesley were fast asleep in the first tent. Coy and Sara joined them and quickly fell asleep as well. In the other tent Jade and William cuddled as Michelle and Tabby talked.

"Where is Kiya?" Tabitha asked.

"She probably just wants to be alone for awhile," Michelle answered. "She just lost her best friend. It has to be hard on her. I couldn't imagine losing you, Tabby."

"I know; I couldn't bear losing you either Shelly."

"I'm going to go check on her," Michelle said. She walked outside and walked over to Kiya who was sitting on the sand with her head down in her hands. "Are you alright?" Michelle asked.

"I don't know. I shouldn't have let him go with us."

"Don't blame yourself. It's not anyone's fault."

"Queen Laza is not going to like the idea that we went to Shondo Waxanadu," Kiya stated.

"So don't tell her," Michelle suggested.

"No, I must tell her. I must take responsibility for what happened to Jango."

"But it isn't your fault. This was our idea, not yours."

Kiya shook her head. She had to tell Queen Laza. She knew there would be consequences but it was the honorable thing to do.

"Come on," Michelle said. "Let's go to sleep. We'll face Queen Laza tomorrow."

Kiya agreed and they went back to the tent.

10

The next morning was a bright and hot one. The two suns were beating down on the explorers as they packed up the tents and headed for the Dambroo village. After a few hours they exited the desert and entered the forest. They were walking through the forest as two Gallimimus darted past them out of nowhere.

"That can't be good," Jade said. "Run!"

"Drop the rafts," Kiya yelled as they all ran. There were thunderous footsteps approaching from behind them. Kiya led them to a row of bushes. Everyone quickly slid behind the bushes and crouched down. A T-Rex quickly ran by them still searching for the Gallimimus which were long gone at this point. They waited a few minutes until Kiya said it was safe. Then, they grabbed the rafts and continued on to the Dambroo village.

Chapter Eighteen:
Consequences

1

They arrived at the Dambroo village and were greeted by the guards. Michelle and Tabitha took Tuni's raft back to him while O'Dell and Sara took Kolani's raft back to him. Wesley and Coy placed Jango's raft by his hut. Michelle and Tabitha placed Tuni's raft outside his hut. They entered as Tuni was eating.

"Dako," Michelle said. Tuni rambled off a sentence in Dambroo.

"Gula Dako," Tabitha said which meant 'no thank you'. They left the hut and headed back to the others.

"What did he say?" Michelle asked.

"He offered us supper," Tabitha answered.

"Oh, that was nice."

Michael and Sara arrived at Kolani's hut, but he wasn't home. They leaned his raft against the hut and returned to the others.

Kiya waited outside of Queen Laza's throne room with the explorers.

"I have to tell Queen Laza," she said.

"We'll go with you," Michelle suggested.

"Are you sure?" Kiya asked.

"Yes," Michelle answered. "It wasn't your idea to go to Shondo Waxanadu, it was ours."

2

They all entered and approached Queen Laza's throne. The queen looked inquisitively at Kiya. Kiya knew at this point the queen had an idea about what had happened. The talk had traveled through the village that the American's and Kiya had borrowed three rafts and Jango had gone with them.

"Shono Jango?" Queen Laza asked.

Kiya had a tear in her eye as she answered the queen. "Wano ju sufo tai Makai de Shondo Waxanadu," she answered. Despite their limited Dambroo, the explorers knew exactly what was being said.

The queen's eyes showed anger. "Shondo Waxanadu?" Queen Laza yelled. "Sarto tai ne mafo Shondo Waxanadu!"

"Tabby?" Michelle asked.

"She is telling Kiya that she's not supposed to go to Shondo Waxanadu," Tabitha translated.

"Ono de sai Jango tono!" the queen rampaged. "Mai tai sarto kuna jen pana nonai. Dambroo sai te woma sarto ne boo sarto fe sonara mainest tona kai wakai."

"Oh no," Tabby said as Kiya began crying.

"What?" Michelle asked.

"The queen said, 'you and your friends are now banished. The Dambroo will not show you hostility, but you and your friends are no longer welcome here.' I feel awful."

"Kiya, I'm sorry," Michelle said.

"No, that's okay. I just need some time," Kiya replied as she ran away.

"Where is she going?" Sara asked.

"I don't know," Tabitha said. "She'll come back to us when she's ready." They all sadly left the village, knowing they were never to return.

3

They did their usual for the next three days with one exception; Kiya was not there to help them. Tabitha started to get worried. "I wonder where she is?"

"I'm sure she's safe," Michelle said. "She's made it out here for this long."

"I know. I guess I just miss her. What is she going to do? She was kicked out of her home."

"Yeah, but she can just live with us like she's been doing," Michelle suggested.

"I don't know about you, but I plan to leave here someday," Sara interjected.

"Yes, I do too," Michelle answered. "But this place is like a paradise. Every day is usually warm. It rarely rains, but rains enough to keep the flora looking beautiful. It has marvelous scenery, unimpeded by humans. It holds many of the same qualities that I enjoyed about the Masai Mara."

"Except it is highly dangerous and we barely get by every day," Tabby said.

"Well, yes. I guess there's that side of it too," Michelle answered with a smile.

4

Back in the ship, O'Dell approached Tom. "I don't want to scare the others, but we're down to eleven shells for the gun. I'm going out hunting today with the spear."

"Good idea," Tom said. "I think we will keep the ammo for a special occasion."

O'Dell went outside and began to walk towards the woods. Sara caught up to him and joined him hunting.

"Are you upset that I dragged you on this mission?" she asked.

"No. I'll only be upset if I don't make it home to enjoy my million dollars."

"It's ironic isn't it? I own an airport with all the fuel I could ever need, but we're stranded here because we have no fuel."

"Well we should have planned better," O'Dell stated. "I don't think any of us realistically expected to find a planet with life on it. Hell, some of us probably didn't even expect to get out of Earth's atmosphere."

"I think we all joined this mission because it was a chance to get away from the real world for awhile. Coy, Paul, and Tom, away from their jobs. Jade away from fighting; I guess I ruined that for her," Sara giggled. "Tabitha and Michelle away from their research. William tried to get away from his unsuccessful paper. Wesley was trying to get away from flying people around. Steve away from the restaurant. I tried to escape the memory of my father's death. That didn't happen. And you tried to escape your conscience."

"My conscience?" Michael asked.

"Yeah. It can't be easy to have a job where you kill defenseless aliens who mean no harm but are just trying to communicate."

"I did what I was told. I did what I had to. What do you know?" O'Dell snapped.

"I know that saying you were just doing your job doesn't make the guilt disappear," Sara replied.

"Maybe not, but it makes me feel better about myself so I can sleep at night."

5

"Look," Sara whispered as she pointed. "There's a deer." It was a little ways away from them. Michael motioned for Sara to stay put as he snuck closer. When he got within twenty feet he launched the spear. The spear hit the doe in the shoulder and went in quite far. The deer stumbled a few steps and fell. Michael ran over and jumped on it before it could get up. He pulled his knife out and cut its throat. The deer let out a gargled snort as Michael got up and backed away. Sara ran over and watched. This scene was almost too violent for her. She felt bad for the deer. The deer lay there panting as blood oozed from its neck. She knelt next to it and put her hand on the deer's chest. She felt it rising and dropping from the deer's breathing. The deer was looking at her. This bothered Sara. She felt awful but knew that they had to eat. She wanted to comfort the deer as much as she could in its last moments. Finally the chest dropped one last time without rising. Michael came over and began to gut it.

"Can't you do that back at the ship?" Sara asked.

"First of all, gutting it will make it lighter," O'Dell mentioned. "We can travel a lot faster with a lighter load to carry. This will help us because we need to move fast. There are probably Raptors coming." He pulled out the intestines.

"What do you mean there are Raptors coming?" Sara asked.

"Didn't you hear the deer snort? I'm sure the Raptors heard it. Let's hope they get full on the guts we're leaving them."

"Oh, I see," Sara said. She grabbed the back legs and Michael grabbed the front as they quickly headed back toward camp.

6

Jade and William left the ship to get sticks and twigs for the fire.

"Do you think we will ever make it home?" Jade asked.

"I don't know, but if we do I'll take you on a real date where you don't have to fetch wood and look out for Raptors." He kissed her and they briefly embraced. They quickly grabbed as many branches and sticks they could find. They headed back to the ship and helped Tom and Coy with the fire. As soon as the fire was started, Coy looked up to see Sara and O'Dell exiting the woods carrying the doe.

"I'm going to go help them," Coy said. Wesley joined him.

"Good job guys," Wesley said as they approached. Coy and Wesley relieved Sara and Michael. They carried the deer back to camp. They cooked the deer and began to eat. During supper they were greeted by a couple Struthiomimus who decided to graze in the field about twenty feet from them. It was a sign of mutual respect. The explorers and Struthiomimus were both eating in the same area knowing they were not a threat to each other.

'This must be what all those herbivores feel like in the Great Plains; Coexisting peacefully with a watchful eye for their common enemy,' Michelle thought.

7

After supper it was getting dark and the Struthiomimus had left.

"Look," Sara said as she pointed toward a bright green glow coming toward them. It was the lightning bugs again. Everyone gathered and watched the luminous show. They let the fire go out as the only light was coming from the bright green glow of the giant bugs overhead.

"This is so beautiful," Sara said.

The swarm of lights was coming to an end. There was one lone lightning bug left trailing the rest. They watched as this final light crossed through the sky above the field. Suddenly that light was violently taken out of the sky.

"Raptors!" O'Dell yelled. "Everyone inside!" They scrambled and hurried inside. They hadn't even seen the Raptors because the light had drawn their attention away from ground level. When everyone was inside William looked out through the camera screen.

"One, two, three, four," he counted. "No wait. Five. Five Raptors! We were lucky."

"We should've been more careful," O'Dell said. "Another few seconds and there would be one less of us."

"Kiya would have known there were Raptors around," Tabitha said. "As long as she's not here, we need to be careful." Everyone went to bed hoping Kiya would return tomorrow.

8

The night ended and morning came. Everyone was sitting around the fire pit. Wesley had even awoken early this morning.

"Professor, should we go looking for Kiya?" Tabitha asked.

"I think she will come back to us when she's ready," he replied.

"But it's been four days. I'm a little worried for her safety."

"My dear," Tom said with a smile. "Kiya is a true warrior. She has beaten all odds to stay alive this long. She is more than capable of taking care of herself out here. I'm not too worried for her safety. Us on the other hand, will struggle without her. She is one of the reasons most of us are still alive. We need her more than she needs us."

9

"Look everyone," William shouted. It was Kiya, coming from the forest. She was carrying breakfast too; a nice sized rabbit. Tabitha ran over to her and hugged her.

"We were worried about you," Tabby said. "Where were you?"

"I was finding my thoughts," Kiya answered. "I needed time to reflect and put Jango's death behind me."

"Well it's good to have you back," Tabitha said. Everyone sat around the campfire in a cheerful mood. They cooked breakfast and chatted.

"Sara," Jade said. "If we make it home..."

"When we make it home," William interrupted.

"Okay, when we make it home," Jade said with a smile, "what are you going to do with the million dollars that you offered Steve and Paul?"

"I've thought about that quite a bit actually," Sara said. "I think I'm going to start a Culinary Arts Scholarship in Steve's name and a Geology scholarship in Paul's name. That is what they loved so I want to spend their money in a way that they would approve of."

"I think that's a splendid idea," Simonson stated.

"What about you Jade," Sara asked. "What are you going to do with your money?"

"What money?" Jade answered. "I didn't come along for the money. I turned you down, remember?"

"Yeah, I remember. But I feel that you deserve it for going through all this and putting up with me," Sara responded.

"William is getting a million dollars, I'll just spend his," she said as they laughed. "Besides, I don't exactly see a way out of here."

"I know," Sara said. "I feel responsible for dragging everyone out here and now we're stranded."

"It's not your fault," Jade said. "Besides, most of us didn't expect to actually find a planet with life. Despite our setbacks, this mission has been a successful one."

"By golly it has been more than just successful," Tom added. "This mission has been the most successful discovery in history. We will be as famous as Galileo, Darwin, and Columbus! This will be in the history books everywhere."

"Only if we get home," Sara stated.

"We'll find a way," Tom said.

10

"Hey, why don't we all go swimming as a group?" Michelle asked. "Anyone interested?"

"I'm up for a swim," Tabby said.

"Yeah, I'm filthy," Sara said.

They all agreed and started walking to the stream.

"Are you guys going to behave this time?" William whispered to Michelle and Tabitha.

"I am," Michelle said. Tom is like a father to me. The last thing I want is for him to see me naked."

"What about you, Tabby?" he asked.

"I didn't want to skinny-dip last time. It was peer pressure," she said with a smile.

When they all arrived at the stream the mood was peaceful and relaxing as they all cleaned up and talked.

William pulled Jade aside to talk to her. "So what are you going to do if we get home?" he asked.

"What do you mean?"

"I mean, will we still be together?" he asked.

"Yeah, and I'll still be a kick boxer and you'll still be a journalist. The only difference is that I might actually grant you an interview." Jade smiled at William. "In fact, I'll only grant you interviews. No one else will get the inside scoop."

"So I'll be able to get up close and personal with you?" he asked with a grin.

She pulled him close to her and wrapped her arms around him. "As close as you get here. But don't print your private life with me okay."

"I wouldn't," he said as they kissed.

"Get a freakin room!" Sara joked.

"I would love that," William said. "Jade honey, want to go check in to the Holiday Inn in the Great Desert or would you prefer the Hilton in the Great Plains?"

11

"Look," Wesley interrupted as he pointed to the sky. Everyone looked up to see a ship landing to the Northeast of them.

"A ship!" Sara yelled. "This is our chance to go home!"

"That looks about where our ship is," Tom said. "If we hurry we can get there in just over an hour. Hopefully it will still be there."

Everyone got out of the water and began to go back toward their ship at a brisk pace.

Chapter Nineteen:
The Return Of Evil

1

When they arrived at the field, the ship was parked right next to theirs.

"It's The Collector," Kiya said. "He's back."

"How do you know?" O'Dell asked.

"I'd recognize that ship anywhere."

"She's right," Tabitha said.

"Well, we have to try to steal his ship," Tom suggested.

"Should we go pack?" William asked.

"No, we have to make sure it's secure first," O'Dell said.

They all cautiously approached the ship. The door was left wide open.

"Why would Arnemore leave the door open?" Michelle asked. "Wouldn't he close the door?"

"Not if he wants to trap us," Kiya said.

They all slowly entered and looked around.

"I found something," William said. The others joined him to see a cannibal in a cage.

"Why would he want a Pantoo," Wesley asked.

"He collects people," Kiya said. "All kinds of people."

The Pantoo looked at them with a sense of hope.

"Let's let him out," Michelle said.

"Are you crazy?" Sara said. "He'll attack us."

"I don't think so. Even the Pantoo don't deserve this."

"Hello?" Sara said. "They eat people!"

"And you eat deer. Does that make you any better? I'll bet the deer would be more afraid of us than a Pantoo. Everything is relative. I'm letting him out." Michelle walked over to the panel and found the button that matched the diagram by the cage. She pushed it as the cage lowered. The cannibal smiled at Michelle then ran out the ship's door. The explorers checked the rest of the ship. It was empty. The Collector was nowhere to be found.

"We must hurry," Professor Simonson said. "We don't know how long we have until he returns." Tom approached the control panel with Wesley. Simonson was shaking his head.

"What's wrong?" William asked from across the room.

"This doesn't make any sense. I can't make heads or tails of it."

"Apparently you have to be smarter than a NASA Scientist to figure it out," William joked. Tom slowly turned with a glare of disapproval. He didn't see the humor in the situation. "Sorry," William said softly as he turned with a grimace.

2

"Look at this!" Coy yelled. He had what looked like a little compressor. It had two hoses hooked to it. "It's some kind of a pump?" Coy said.

Tom's eyes lit up. "Can you figure it out, Coy?"

"I think so."

"Great! Let's steal his fuel and pump it into our ship. Will the hoses reach?" Tom asked.

"They look long enough."

"Yes!" Tom shouted.

Everyone was overjoyed. This was their chance to get home. Coy and the others exited the ship and hooked the pump up to Arnemore's ship and theirs. The hoses had more than enough length to accommodate.

"I'm going to get our ship ready for take off," Tom said.

"I'll help," O'Dell said as he joined Tom. Wesley also went with them.

"Kiya, are you going with us?" Michelle asked.

"I don't know."

"You better decide fast," William stated.

"I have no place to stay," she said. "I'm not sure I would be able to adjust to your world. I would be a burden."

"Nonsense," Michelle said. "We have been a burden to you here. It is our turn to take care of you. You have no place to stay here anyway because of us. You can stay with me."

"Are you sure?" Kiya asked.

"Yes, I could use the help," Michelle answered.

"Okay," Kiya agreed.

Outside the pump was hooked up.

"Okay, start it up," Sara said.

"I can't," Coy replied.

"What do you mean you can't?" Sara asked. "Why can't you?"

"There is no start button. It has a receiver here though. There must be a remote to it."

"It must be in the ship," Tabby said. "Come on."

3

Tom, Wesley, and O'Dell were still preparing their ship as the others ran into The Collector's ship to look for the remote. Everyone was searching different rooms. Tabby saw it in the room she was searching. It was on a pedestal. Next to it was The Collector. He returned while everyone was outside connecting the pump. *'He didn't have time,'* she thought. *'We would have heard him. Kiya would have heard him. How did he get back so fast. It's like he just appeared.'* The Collector smiled at her.

"In here!" Tabitha yelled as she ran across the room toward the remote.

Arnemore began to push several buttons on the wall. The floor dropped all around her and water surrounded the pedestal she was on. The others entered the room to see the water in front of them in a pool. Tabby was in the middle on an island and Arnemore was on the far end next to the wall. He was also raised out of the water by a pedestal, which held that very important remote.

"It's over there guys," Tabitha said as she pointed. Arnemore pushed another button and a second liquid entered the water through little holes in the walls.

"Shosho Coolon," Arnemore said as he laughed.

"Don't touch the water!" Kiya yelled. "It's poisonous."

"Kiya, what does Shosho mean," Tabby asked. "I know Coolon is poison."

"Shosho is a type of snake here. It spits poison at its prey. The poison soaks in through your skin and kills you within minutes. If it gets in your mouth it only takes seconds to kill you."

"Sounds like a form of spitting cobra," Michelle said.

"There's no way to get the remote," Kiya said. "The poison will kill you, Tabby."

"We'll have to find another way," Michele said.

"There is no other way," Tabitha said. "I love you guys." She jumped into the water and ran toward Arnemore and the remote.

"Tabby, no!" Michelle screamed. "What are you doing?" Arnemore was surprised. He didn't expect her to sacrifice herself for the others. Tabitha bent down and scooped some of the poisonous water into her hand and threw it at The Collector. Arnemore tried to shield himself but failed. "Ahh!" he screamed as the liquid hit his eyes and he fell to the ground. His body started convulsing and then suddenly stopped.

"Tabby, no," Michelle sobbed. Tabby grabbed the remote.

"Catch," she yelled as she tossed it across the room. William grabbed it.

"I love you guys," she said "Thank you for the best time of my life. You all became my best fiends."

"Tabby I love you," Michelle cried.

"I know Shelly. Good lu…" she fell down in the water and went into convulsions.

"No!" Michelle yelled as she lunged forward. Kiya grabbed her and held her away from the ledge.

"It's too late," Kiya said. Michelle turned and hugged Kiya.

4

William and Coy took the remote outside and started up the pump. O'Dell and Wesley exited the other ship and joined them.

"The ship is ready," O'Dell said. "We're just waiting for fuel."

"Is everything okay," Wesley asked as he saw a tear rolling down William's cheek.

"No," William said.

"What? Is The Collector back?" O'Dell asked.

"We don't have to worry about him anymore," Coy said. "Tabitha took him out, but she took her own life at the same time."

"No, are you sure," O'Dell asked.

"Yeah," William said softly.

"No," Wesley said as he shook his head in disbelief. "No, damn it!"

"Is Michelle okay?" O'Dell asked.

"She's taking it hard," William said. "The girls are with her."

"We're full," Coy said as he disconnected the pump.

5

Everyone gathered outside except Tom who was still in the other ship. Michelle was standing with one arm around Jade and the other around Sara. They were comforting her.

"Are we ready?" O'Dell asked.

"We're set," Coy said.

William took the pump inside their ship and approached Tom. "Tom, I've got some bad news."

"What? The pump won't work?" Simonson asked.

"No. The pump is fine. We're full of fuel."

"Great, then what's wrong?"

"We lost Tabitha," William said.

"Where is she?" Tom asked.

"No," William said. "I mean she died."

"How in the world did that happen?" Tom asked.

"The Collector came back and Tabitha sacrificed herself so we could get the remote for the pump. She killed The Collector, but was poisoned and died. She is the reason we can go home."

"Is Michelle alright?" Tom asked.

"She's a little shaken up," William responded.

Tom ran out and hugged Michelle. "Oh my dear, I'm so sorry." William walked out and put his arms around Jade.

"The navigational system is up and running," said Professor Simonson. "We can board when everyone's ready.

6

"Tuni," Kiya yelled as she looked across the field to see him jogging toward their ship. He approached them and spoke to Kiya in Dambroo.

"We saw the ship," he said. "I was sent ahead to scout."

"It was The Collector," Kiya said. "He is no longer. I'm leaving with the explorers. Tell everyone that I'm sorry and I'll miss them."

Tuni hugged her. "Good luck," he said as he turned and walked away.

"I think we should all board soon," Tom said. "Everyone take one last look before we leave."

O'Dell and Coy walked over to the ship's door and turned back to face the field. "No more eating Compies," Coy said.

"Or running from Raptors," O'Dell added. They turned and entered the ship.

Wesley was the next to enter. *'No more fetching water,'* he thought.

Jade and William walked up to the door hand in hand. "I'm glad this hell is over," Jade said.

"Hell? This has been the best time of my life," William said. "I met the girl of my dreams."

"You journalists will say anything to get an interview won't you?" Jade said as they laughed and entered.

Sara was next. She walked to the door as a tear rolled down her face. She was actually sad to be leaving. She was leaving an adventure where she was surrounded by people who cared more about her and less about her money. She was able to escape the loss of her father for a little while but now she was returning home to an empty house.

Michelle hugged Kiya. "You can stay with me now," Michelle said.

"I know. I'm excited. Your world is going to be difficult for me to adjust to though. I'll need you to protect me."

"I'll be right there with you," Michelle said. She walked up to the door and paused for a moment to reflect. *'I'll never forget you Tabby,'* she thought. *'You are the reason we are all going home. Thank you!'*

Kiya approached the door as Michelle entered the ship. She turned to take one last look at her world. *'Jango, I'm sorry. I'll always think of you. You will always be in my heart as will the Dambroo village. But I must start my new life now in a new world with my new friends.'*

Tom was the last one outside. He looked across the field as two Gallimimus jogged across. He looked up one final time at the beautiful horizon with its two suns. *'This mission has been a success despite the loss of some of our friends. I'll make sure that their deaths weren't in vain. I'll miss this enchanted planet, but perhaps we'll make it back here some day.'* He turned and entered the ship. Everyone took their spots as they prepared to launch.

7

"Is everyone ready?" Tom asked. "Here we go!" The ship slowly rose from the field as the Gallimimus ran off. As they ascended a T-Rex entered the field and let out a roar. They were safely off the planet now.

"I'm flying," Kiya said with a smile on her face. Except for jumping, she had never been off the ground before. It was a unique feeling for her.

"Yes, we are all flying my dear," Tom replied. "Once again, we'll work in shifts. I'll take Coy, Sara, Jade, and William. Shift two will be Michael, Wesley, Kiya, and Michelle. You may all go rest now if you like."

Kiya was interested in watching the screen and stayed out with Tom and Coy. The rest of shift two went in to sleep. The crews switched every twelve hours and they had a rather safe trip. The meteor belt posed no problems except the constant pounding that Sara had almost forgotten about. Everyone was awake as they were approaching Earth.

"Look," Michelle said. "Isn't it beautiful?"

"That is the most beautiful thing I've ever seen," Wesley said. "I didn't think we would ever see it again." Tears began to flow from everyone.

"That is your home?" Kiya asked.

"Yes, this is our wakai," Michelle said.

"It is beautiful." Kiya agreed.

"Kiya, I'm going to make your transition to our planet easier," Sara said. "I'm going to give you a million dollars too. You suffered on this mission as much as the rest of us."

"What are dollars?" Kiya asked.

"It is money," Michelle said.

"Is money important?" Kiya asked.

"Not as important as friendship," Sara said. "But it sure helps."

"Okay, then thank you," Kiya smiled.

Kiya had already begun to wear Michelle's cloths because she was told the deer fur would be a give away that she was not from Earth, or if she was she was a wacko.

Chapter Twenty:
Return To Earth

1

"Can we land at my airport?" Sara asked.

"As long as we don't get shot down," O'Dell said. "Our military might be tracking us as we speak." As they descended toward the Allison Smith Memorial Airport William gazed at the camera screen.

"We've got company," he said.

"How many?" O'Dell asked.

"Looks like two jets."

"Okay, everyone strap in. They will take us out," Michael said.

"I still think I'll be able to land this bad boy," Wesley commented.

"I hope so," Sara said as she looked over at Kiya clutching her chair in fear. She had never dealt with a situation like this and was unsure how safe she was. *'What if the people of this planet realize I'm not from here,'* she thought. *'They might imprison me.'* She knew that Michelle and the others would try to protect her but what if they couldn't.

"Now listen," O'Dell said. "Everyone stay in the ship once we have landed. They have been trained to shoot anything that comes out."

Everyone was strapped in and prepared to be shot down. A sudden blast jolted the rear of the ship.

"They hit us," O'Dell said.

"We're going down," Wesley added. "Hold on." They plummeted fast as the two fighter jets pulled up into the clouds.

2

The ground was advancing quickly. William and Jade held each other's hands tightly. After everything they had fought through, this should not be the way they die. Wesley was able to level the ship off just above the runway. It crashed down lightly and skidded a little before coming to rest. The landing was rocky but everyone was relieved that they were safe for the moment.

"There's troops," William said as everyone looked out the ship's camera screen. There were several men parachuting down to the runway. The scene reminded Sara of the day she met O'Dell. All these troops landed and he was the only one that survived. Then he faced all the dangers of the new planet and he lived through that as well. He truly was a soldier. They all were in a way.

William could see the troops landing and surrounding the ship with their guns raised. O'Dell pushed the button for the door to open. They all stayed out of sight as the door opened. The troops in front of the door prepared themselves.

"I'm going to go talk to them," O'Dell said. "Everyone stay here." Everyone was unstrapped now and watched eagerly on the camera screen.

"Does everyone on your planet have these awful guns?" Kiya asked.

"Well, most people own one," Michelle answered. "This is our military though. They are our warriors. They protect us."

"They don't look like they want to protect us," Kiya said.

3

Michael crept up until he was by the door but still out of sight. "American!" he yelled out. "We are American." Some of the soldiers lowered their guns.

"Keep your aim," their Sergeant yelled. "We don't know if they are human. Those aliens are intelligent and might have learned our language." The troops raised their guns again. "How many aboard?" the Sergeant asked.

"Nine," O'Dell replied.

"Do you nine have names?"

"Yes sir we do," Michael answered. "My name is Michael O'Dell." The Sergeant recognized the name right away. Michael O'Dell was one of the men sent to recover the last alien ship. No one returned from that mission. The rest of the men on that day had been identified by dental records and DNA but Michael O'Dell's body was never found. It was thought that the aliens abducted him on that day when the ship disappeared. The Sergeant was still a little leery.

"Michael," he said. "Are there any aliens on board?"

Michael was worried that they would ask about Kiya. He knew however, that by aliens the Sergeant meant little gray men. Kiya looked as much like them as any normal person would.

"No! No aliens," O'Dell responded.

"Michael, I want you and only you to step off the ship. I want you to move slowly with your hands up. Do you understand?"

"Yes, understood sir," he said as he slowly walked off the ship. He carried the gun with him but tossed it on the ground as he exited the ship. One soldier ran up and began to pat him down.

"I have a knife strapped to my leg," O'Dell mentioned to the soldier.

"Which leg?" the soldier asked.

"Right."

The soldier rolled up O'Dell's pants and unstrapped the knife. "Thank you," he said.

"No problem. We just don't want you to think we are aliens."

"You should be alright," the soldier said. "This is just a precaution." The soldier led O'Dell to the Sergeant.

"Hello Mr. O'Dell," the Sergeant said. "Are you okay?"

"Yes."

"What about your crew inside?"

"They are fine also, sir."

"Who is on board the ship?" the Sergeant asked.

"Professor Tom Simonson, Coy Riggs, Wesley Sparks, William Day, Sara Smith, Jade Evans, Michelle Austin, and …" O'Dell thought for a second. "Kiya Austin, Michelle's sister."

"Okay, now do you want to explain what happened?"

"I think you would get a better answer from Professor Simonson or Sara Smith," Michael said.

"Can you call them out for us?" the Sergeant asked.

"I don't want them harmed," O'Dell said as he looked over at the soldiers who still had their guns pointed toward the ship's door.

"They won't be harmed," the Sergeant said. "This is just precaution. You know that."

"Sara and Tom," O'Dell yelled. "They want you to come out next. Keep your hands up." Sara and Tom walked to the door.

4

Kiya was a little worried now. "What are they doing?" she asked. "Why can't we all get off? Do they know that I'm not an American?"

"Relax," Michelle said. "I won't let anything happen to you."

Sara and Tom walked down and got searched by the soldiers. The Sergeant motioned for them to come over to him.

"So you said there are nine of you?" the Sergeant asked O'Dell again.

"Yes, nine of us," O'Dell answered.

"Professor Tom Simonson," Tom said as he approached them with his hand out.

"And I presume you're Sara Smith," the Sergeant said. Sara nodded. "I'm Sergeant Joseph Smalt. Nice to meet you. Now, do you want to explain to me what you are doing in an alien ship?"

"The ship crashed here at my airport," Sara explained. "We fixed it up and used it."

"Used it for what?" Sergeant Smalt asked.

"We used it to travel into space and explore the possibility of life out there," Simonson responded.

"Really, did you find anything interesting?" Sergeant Smalt joked.

"Oh yes," Simonson answered. "A marvelous planet with tremendous plant and animal life.

"You're serious?"

"Oh yes. It was amazing," Simonson said.

"Well the government will have to decide what to do with the ship."

"We would prefer to keep the ship," Simonson said.

"I'm sure the government doesn't want anyone to know about this planet that you supposedly went to. For now, the ship can stay here. This airport isn't to be used and the ship has to remain a secret for now; is that understood?"

"Yes," Tom agreed. "Can the others exit now?"

"Yes, single file with their hands up."

O'Dell called for the others to exit the ship.

"We can exit now," William said.

"What if they find out I'm not from here?" Kiya asked.

"Relax," Michelle said. "They won't know." They all exited the ship and were searched. After some interrogation, the troops left and everyone went in the house.

"Well everyone, we completed our mission," Tom said with a smile. "I have a lot of work to do now so I must be returning home."

"Work or bragging, Professor?" William asked.

"Well, I have a lot of bragging to do as well. Thank you all."

"Professor," Sara said. "I would have Wesley fly you home with my jet but we're not supposed to use the airport."

"Oh that's alright. I was just going to call a cab to take me to the airport."

"No, I'll call Peter my limo driver. He has to come with the money anyways. I want to settle my debts to everyone."

Sara picked up the phone and dialed Peter's number.

"Hello," he said.

"Peter?"

"Yes, who's this?" he questioned.

"You don't recognize my voice? Has it been that long?" Sara asked.

"Sara?"

"Yes, we're home"

"Sara is that really you. I was wondering when I would hear from you. No phone calls or anything."

"I know, I couldn't call. Is my account okay? Did Sylvia let you manage it?" Sara asked.

"I took care of everything," Peter said.

"Great. Can you come to the airport? Can you withdraw eight million dollars?"

"Eight million dollars? Are you crazy?"

"Yes I'm crazy," Sara said. "I need eight million dollars. You have always been a trustworthy employee of my father's. I wouldn't ask anyone else."

"Okay, it might take awhile for the bank to provide that amount of money,"

"They should have no trouble," Sara said. "My father set up a special deal with them to always have ten million available at all times. He wanted to be able to have that money set aside in case of an emergency."

"Ten million? That is one hell of an emergency fund."

"You know dad, he always over plans."

"Okay, I'll be there in an hour or two."

"Thanks, bye Peter."

"Really it's no trouble for me to call a cab," Tom said.

"Well, this way I can pay everyone as well," Sara said.

5

Kiya was amazed at her new home. She looked around and studied everything.

"Look," she said as she pointed to a bird.

"Yeah so," William said.

"What is it?" Kiya asked.

"It's a robin," Michelle said.

"My planet didn't have robins. Ooh! Pretty one!" Kiya said as she pointed again.

"That's a blue jay," Michelle said.

"Look," Kiya said as she pointed up to a passing plane. "Visitors. Let's go see who it is." Everyone chuckled.

"What? They could be bad?" Kiya asked.

"There are planes in the sky all the time," William explained. "That is how we get from place to place."

Kiya looked confused. "You don't walk?"

"Short distances, but we fly to other cities," William said.

"Kiya our planet has much more land than yours," Tom said. "As amazed as we were with your planet, you will certainly be more astounded at ours. I guess we really have taken this place for granted."

Everyone sat around and chatted until Peter pulled up in the limo.

"What's that?" Kiya asked.

"That's my friend Peter," Sara said.

"No, I think she means the car," William said. "That is another way we travel."

Peter got out of the car and hugged Sara. "I'm glad you are okay," he said.

"Did you have any trouble with the money?" Sara asked.

"No, I didn't once I said *little devil*."

"Great," Sara said as Peter handed her a briefcase from the back of the limo. There were several lying on the seat.

"Each one has a million?" Sara asked.

"Yes, the bank put them in separate briefcases," Peter said.

"Great," Sara said. "This is for you Tom," she said as she handed him a briefcase."

"I told you that I didn't need your money," Tom said. "I did this for the adventure and growth of scientific knowledge."

"I know," Sara said. "But this is something I must do. Please accept it."

Tom smiled and grabbed the case.

"Peter, can you take Tom to the airport?"

"We're at the airport," he replied.

"I know. I mean a different airport. We can't use this one. It's a long story."

Peter nodded as Tom walked over to the others.

"Wesley, it has been a pleasure flying with you."

"Likewise Professor," Wesley replied as they shook hands.

"Jade and William, I wish you the best of luck in the future."

"Thanks," they said in unison.

"Michael, you kept us all alive as much as Kiya did. Thank you for being the true soldier that you are."

"You all were one great set of troops," O'Dell said with a smile.

"Kiya," Tom said. "I wish you the best of luck in our world. Michelle is a great person and I think you will have a great time staying with her. You were very instrumental in saving us and I just want to say thanks. I know that you gave up a lot for us."

"You're welcome," Kiya said as she hugged him.

"Sara, if it weren't for you we would never had this marvelous opportunity. Your father has a lot to be proud of."

Sara hugged him as a tear ran down her cheek.

"Coy, you're a good man. You deserve a million dollars as much as anyone I know. Put it to good use son."

"I will Professor," Coy said. "I owe it all to you though. If it weren't for you I wouldn't have even been considered for this mission."

"Coy, I didn't recommend you as a favor. I did it because we needed you." Coy smiled as they shook hands.

Michelle ran up to Tom and hugged him. "Sweetie, I know how much you want to help your wildlife program. But try to be a little selfish. Spend some of your money on yourself okay. You deserve it."

"I will."

"And you know if you ever need anything, I'm only a phone call away." Tom got into the car as Peter unloaded the rest of the briefcases. Peter gave them all a wave before entering the car and driving off.

6

Sara handed everyone their briefcases as they all went inside. Jade was the only person who refused money. Sara kept insisting but Jade would not allow it. They all talked most of the night before turning in. The next morning was the time for everyone to depart. Sara had called Peter who was going to transport everyone outside the airport where she had separate limos waiting for everyone. This way the drivers were unaware of the alien ship that sat on the runway. O'Dell, Wesley, and Coy were first. They said goodbye to everyone and entered the limo with Peter. Kiya and Michelle were next. They hugged Sara, William, and Jade before leaving as well.

"What about you two?" Sara asked. "Are you going to the city or Jade's little town?"

"I think we can go to the city so William can check on his paper," Jade replied.

"Guys, I'm so sorry," Sara said. "I put you two through hell. You are the best friends I've ever had."

"Sadly, even including all the bad stuff you've done you are still the best friend I ever had too," Jade said. She hugged Sara. "If you ever need anything, call."

"I will," Sara said as she hugged William. "You two had better stay together."

"If we could make it through what we've already made it through, we should be okay," William said.

They too left as Sara spent the day alone at the airport before returning home the next day.

7

Two years had now passed since their glorious return to Earth. Wesley Sparks opened a pilot's school with his money. He enjoyed flying and visited the others often, still using the occasional Sweet Cheeks title for Sara with no prevail.

Michael O'Dell was discharged from the military. He was tried before a military tribunal where his peers felt his amazing accomplishments far outweighed his disobeying orders and procedures. He was given an honorable discharge and now lives in Gulf Breeze Florida. He makes the short flight from Pensacola to Miami once a week to visit his mother and his brother Jordan. He has become a volunteer firefighter which he enjoys very much. It is his true love of helping others and making them feel secure that allows him to succeed in whatever he does.

Professor Tom Simonson has become world renown for the expedition. While some still believe it is a hoax, he has done several news and talk shows. He has talked about a return expedition but nothing is in the works yet.

Michelle Austin still has her captive breeding program which has become very successful. She still does Safari tours to show people the true beauty of the Masai Mara and its wildlife.

Kiya is now known as Kiya Austin. She still lives with Michelle and helps her on a daily basis. Professor Simonson was right. The beauty of Earth has overwhelmed her. She has grown to love the cat family just as Michelle does. She has adapted well and has even done Safari tours on her own when Michelle wasn't feeling up to it. All the explorers made a pact to keep Kiya's identity a secret. They have all lived up to that.

Coy Riggs has quit his job and become the new manager of a car dealership; the same exact dealership that belongs to Sara Smith. He enjoys being his own boss and Sara allows him the freedom to run things the way he likes.

Sara Smith has set up the Steve Hanson Culinary Arts Scholarship for students that excel in cooking. She has also started the Paul Finch Geology Scholarship for students who enjoy geology. Just last week the finishing touches were done on the Tabitha Jones Memorial Research Center. It is a three million dollar complex in Brazil dedicated to finding a cure for Cancer.

Sara Smith has a new passion these days. She has purchased a small television station where she is a news anchor. Along side of her is William Day. He still has his newspaper, but most of his time goes into helping Sara with the news broadcast. William and Jade are still happily together. There are rumors of a possible marriage next year.

Jade is still a very successful kick boxer. Sara has continuously offered Jade her million dollars from the trip but Jade still refuses. Jade however, did win an invitational kickboxing tournament with sixty four of the worlds best female fighters. The tournament had a million dollar payout from an anonymous backer, that turned out to be Sara Smith.

ABOUT THE AUTHOR

Don Darrin was born in Bath, New York on September 2nd, 1977. He grew up and currently resides in the small town of Pulteney, New York. He went to Hammondsport Central School and Corning Community College. In the summers in Pulteney he runs the Pulteney Youth Basketball Organization, which is a recreational program for the local youth. He enjoys almost all sports. He spends much of his free time with his nieces and nephew. Family is important to him. In his free time he enjoys hiking the local creeks and golfing, poorly I might add. This is his first attempt at writing a book. He hopes to have several more on the way. To him writing is like watching a movie, but you get to decide the ending.

Printed in the United States
65552LVS00001B